STRANGER ON RHANNA

Also by Christine Marion Fraser

CHRISTINE MARION FRASER

Stranger on Rhanna

HarperCollins*Publishers*

HarperCollins*Publishers*
77–85 Fulham Palace Road,
Hammersmith, London W6 8JB

Published by HarperCollins*Publishers* 1992

9 8 7 6 5 4 3 2 1

A catalogue record for this book is
available from the British Library

ISBN 0 00 223813 6

Set in Linotron Times and Janson by
Falcon Typographic Art Ltd, Edinburgh & London

Printed and Bound in Great Britain by
Hartnolls Limited, Bodmin, Cornwall.

For Andy 'Mahatmacoat' McKillop – the best.

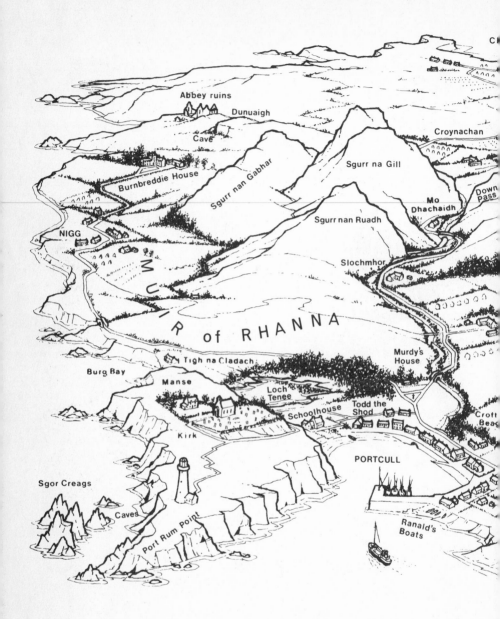

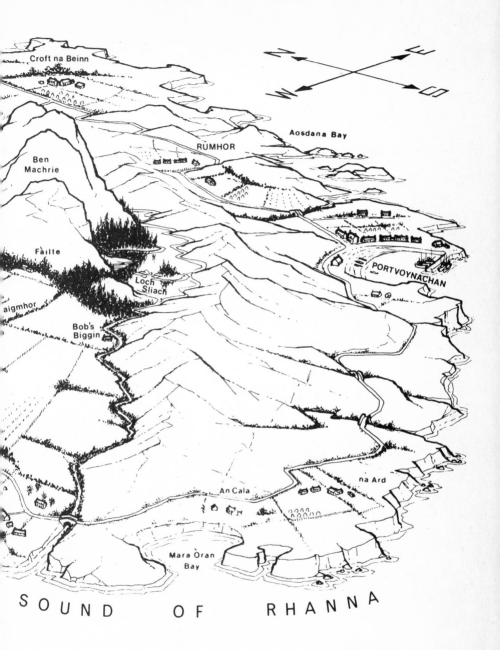

Croft na Beinn

Aosdana Bay

RÙMHOR

Ben
Machrie

Fàilte

Loch
Sliach

PORTVOYNACHAN

aigmhor

Bob's
Biggin

na Ard

An Cala

Mara Òran
Bay

S O U N D   O F   R H A N N A

Part One

SPRING 1967

Chapter One

Rachel stood at the door of An Cala and breathed deeply the scents of sea and machair that were borne to her on the fresh breezes of the early March day. Her dark eyes gazed out to the Sound of Rhanna where lively white sea horses leapt and pranced in foaming turbulence, and she thought how good it was to be back home on Rhanna, listening to the cries of the wheeling gulls and the wild surge of the ocean.

The rest of the world seemed so far away, especially her hectic world of endless concert tours that took her from one country to the next, where she was never still for a moment and there was never any time to pause and remember the people and places that were dear and familiar to her, but which were so very far removed from the bustle, the excitement and the adoring public that demanded so much of her time, her energy, her emotions . . .

Lately it had all become too much for her; she was drained, physically and mentally, and she hadn't made any objections when Jon, her husband, had suggested that she should take a long holiday.

'At least six months,' he had told her firmly. 'You are between tours and deserve a long spell away from it all. You could spend some time on Rhanna, then, if you would like, I'll take you some place where the sun shines all day and all we need to do is eat and sleep and find time for each other again.'

She thought about Jon. He was so good to her: always thinking about her welfare, devoting himself to her every whim, managing her affairs, travelling with her wherever she went.

'Whither thou goest I will go also.'

The words floated into her mind and she smiled because for once Jon hadn't come with her but had instead gone to visit his big, domineering Mamma in Hamburg who had never ceased to be surprised that her son had actually severed the apron strings to marry a girl from a remote Scottish island.

He hadn't suggested that Rachel should accompany him to Hamburg. His monumental Mamma, with her loud, demanding voice, had never taken to Rachel – after all, wasn't she the girl who had stolen away her only son? Never mind that she was a world-famous violinist, at heart she was still as wild and as abandoned as the gypsy-like child he had fallen in love with on a fateful visit to Rhanna many years ago. She didn't have the breeding, she didn't have the poise, she only had her music and she wouldn't have made such a success of that if it hadn't been for Jon's sacrificing his own musical talents so that she could pursue fame and fortune.

Besides all that, she had been born with a terrible physical defect, and no man should have to live with such a thing: it wasn't right, it wasn't normal. Perhaps there were other abnormalities that no one knew about. Why hadn't Rachel conceived by now? She was young, she looked strong enough. It couldn't be Jon's fault: he was healthy and normal. A man needed children to keep him happy. Of course, it might have something to do with all that traipsing about from one country to the next: what sort of a life was that for any married couple? But, of course, Rachel needed the fame, the adoration – never mind her husband and the sacrifices he'd had to make . . .

Jon had heard it all many times and he never exposed Rachel to his mother's narrow reasonings if he could help it. But Rachel knew what Mamma Jodl thought of her: it was all there, in the accusing blue eyes, in the way the woman watched her and made reference to Jon's forebears.

'There has always been a son to carry on the name of Jodl,' she would say with calculating nonchalance. 'We are a family who go back a long way, and always there is the strong seed, the male line. Jon would never deliberately allow it to die out, he has always been proud of his name.'

But Mamma Jodl was very far from Rachel's mind that crisp, bright March day with Mara Òran Bay sparkling at her feet and the great dome of the sky stretching wide and infinite overhead. She had been on the island two days now but no one knew that she was here: she had wanted time to be alone, just herself and the silence, the blessed, wondrous silence she had dreamed about for so long. It was a reprieve from people. A blissful respite from hurry, noise, bustle, and – most importantly – there was no phone. At their flat in London they were besieged with requests for her presence at many and varied functions; they were inundated with mail; the door went; the phone jangled. It was an exciting but exhausting life and when it all became too much she knew she had to escape back to the peace and serenity of Rhanna, her island home, her refuge when the bigger world became intolerable.

She had come armed with enough supplies to last several days. On the boat she had worn dark glasses and had kept her coat collar muffled round her face. No one had given her a second glance. It had been a rough crossing from Oban and most of the passengers had sat in the saloon, either 'half asleep or half dead or a mixture o' both', according to Ranald who had been over on the mainland visiting one of his many cousins.

'Ay, well, if that's the case, I'd rather be dying wi' a good tot o' rum in me,' Captain Mac had returned and so saying he had staggered off in the direction of the bar, clutching an assortment of parcels, with Ranald so close on his heels that he had tripped and half fallen out of the doorway, leaving behind him a string of oaths that could only have come from a man who had spent most of his life at sea.

The expletives were like music in Rachel's ears. She had half thought of joining the two men in the bar but had quickly decided against it. Word of her arrival would spread round the island like wildfire and, until she was settled, that was the last thing she wanted.

No one had noticed her leaving the boat and she had been able to make her leisurely way to An Cala, observed only by the sheep cropping the machair and three large Highland cows, who had gazed at her benignly through untidy straggles of wheat-coloured hair.

It had been wonderful to be alone in An Cala – which was the Gaelic for The Haven or The Harbour – no one but herself, wandering through the quiet rooms, every window affording views of sea and shore, hills and fields.

Heating had been a problem. She hadn't wanted to broadcast her presence by having smoke blowing from the chimneys, so she compromised by lighting the fire only at night and by day keeping herself so busy cleaning the house she had no time to feel cold. Of course, she could have started the generator that supplied An Cala with electric heat and light, but the road was nearby, as was Croft na Ard, the home of Anton and Babbie Büttger. Anybody could have heard the rather noisy generator purring away in its shed, so she had cooked her meals on the Calor-gas stove and had eaten them curled up by the fire with the curtains pulled across the windows. Candles and oil lamps allowed her to read and light her way to bed and it had altogether been two of the most relaxing days she had spent for years.

She knew, of course, that she must soon make her presence known – the Rhanna folk didn't appreciate such secrecy and when they found out she had slipped on to the island without anyone knowing she would be the talk of the place. Behag Beag and Elspeth Morrison, in particular, would no doubt have the most to say on the subject. But for now it was enough that she went undiscovered and with an upsurge of sheer abandonment she tossed back her glossy black hair and spread wide her arms as if to embrace the ocean to her breast.

Ruth wandered slowly along the white sands of Mara Òran Bay, deep in thought, in her mind writing the final chapter of her

14

second book. The dialogue was piling in on her and, getting out her notebook, she jotted the words down before they could slip away. Ahead of her, four-and-a-half-year-old Douglas ran and played, his lint-white head bobbing about as he searched for small sea creatures in the rock pools. He was a child who craved perpetual motion and interest in his life. That afternoon he had been particularly restless and in exasperation Ruth had set out to take him for a long walk by the shore, even if it meant leaving her typewriter for a while.

But she was glad that she had come out: Lorn was always telling her that she spent far too much time in the house. Lifting her head, she took a deep breath of salt-laden sea air. Her eyes travelled upwards to An Cala, and she wondered when Rachel would come back to Rhanna. It had been some months since she had seen her friend; she loved it when Jon and Rachel came home, their lives were so exciting and there was always so much they had to tell her – the places they'd seen, the people they'd met . . .

A movement near the house attracted her attention. Shading her eyes, she stared upwards and made out a lone figure standing on the cliffs gazing out to sea. Her heart quickened. It surely couldn't be Rachel: she hadn't written to say she was coming – but who else could be wandering about outside An Cala, if not Rachel?

Calling on Douglas, she hurried with him up the steep track to the house, her violet eyes shining when she saw that it was indeed the girl who, in long-ago childhood, had shared all her little secrets.

'Rachel!' she called breathlessly, running forward as she spoke.

Rachel spun round, her heart galloping into her throat with fright. So engrossed had she been with her thoughts, with the glorious sense of being the only person inhabiting this particular spot at that particular time, she hadn't been aware of any other living soul encroaching on this private place that she considered to be hers.

She loved Ruth, she had always loved her, they had spent the

15

early years of their lives together. She had travelled the world but never had she found anyone who could ever quite compare with Ruth: she could never be as confiding, or as trusting with anyone else, but Ruth could be possessive at times and the way she was feeling now, Rachel didn't want to be possessed by anyone, not even her childhood friend.

Her reciprocal greeting was therefore somewhat restrained and Ruth's face fell a little when her welcoming embrace was not wholeheartedly returned. With the intention of making some excuse to be on her way, she opened her mouth to call on Douglas, but he was already clinging to the hand of the lovely young woman whom he had called 'Aunt Ray' ever since he had learned to speak.

It didn't matter to him that she couldn't answer him back, he simply watched her expressive gestures, the fluent movements of her hands, and gradually he was learning the basic symbols of the sign language.

Rachel led him into the house and Ruth could do nothing but follow, though slowly, indignation growing in her at the realisation that Rachel hadn't told her she was coming to the island – when she had always declared she wouldn't feel right arriving on Rhanna with no Ruth to greet her at the harbour.

The fire was unlit and the house was cold. With a strange little smile, Rachel struck a match and held it to the twists of paper in the grate. She didn't need wood, from an early age she had been taught how to light a fire without it and she had never forgotten the art. She watched the flames curling, the smoke drifting up the chimney. It didn't matter now: she had been discovered, there was no further need to deny herself home comforts, very soon the whole of Rhanna would know that she was here. The solitude, the peace, was over.

'I'll make tea.' Ruth got up and went to the tiny kitchen, her limp pronounced as it always was when she was upset or angry. She rattled cups and saucers with energy, she found the tea caddy and poured hot water into the teapot to warm it. The tea smelled funny, sort of smoky and spicy. Just like Rachel, she thought, even her very tea has to be exotic and different. No wonder Annie, her mother, sometimes said that her daughter's head was too full of fancy ideas for her own good.

When finally she carried the tray of tea and biscuits into the living room, the fire was leaping up the lum and Douglas was ensconced in a big comfortable armchair, happily applying coloured crayons to a picture book on his lap.

Rachel kept a good supply of chalks and children's books in the house for the benefit of young visitors. She was altogether most attentive to their needs, and though each and every one of them knew that she could be as firm as she was kind-hearted, they all respected her for it and were, with few exceptions, as eager to please her as she was them.

There had been a time in her life when she hadn't wanted children but as the years had gone by her attitudes had changed till now she was more than anxious to have a much longed-for baby. It didn't matter that such an event would interrupt her career and she often thought longingly of what it would be like to have the same kind of life as other young married women. But for her it could never be like that and she knew it: her passion for music would never be stilled and always she would strive for perfection till the pinnacle was reached.

Ruth drew in a chair to the fire, smiling a little to herself when she smelled the incense that pervaded the room. Rachel said she burned it to sweeten the air and take away the mustiness from rooms that had lain empty, but the islanders had different ideas. Old Sorcha insisted on calling the strange perfume 'incest' and claimed it made her feel funny whenever she 'sniffed in the reek o' it'. And whenever Kate McKinnon visited her granddaughter she danced and swayed to Rachel's 'provocative oriental music' looking glazed about the eyes, 'as if the incest had seeped into her head and made her think about her essentials', to quote Sorcha.

Rachel had gotten over her annoyance at the intrusion, and she eagerly asked Ruth to relate all her news, her hands and fingers flying so fast they were just a blur of frantic movement. But Ruth had long ago learnt the sign language and was able to answer every question, for although her friend was dumb her hearing was perfect. Nevertheless, many assumed that speech and hearing defects went hand in hand and were quite nonplussed in Rachel's company.

Forgetting her earlier feelings of anger, Ruth explained that she was just finishing her second novel, *The Far Island*, and that the paperback of her first book, *Hebridean Dream*, was due to be released shortly.

Rachel studied her friend – she looked so happy, fair-haired, violet-eyed Ruth, so fragile-seeming with her small-boned figure and the limp that had been her legacy since birth. But Ruth was stronger than she looked: she had triumphed over a difficult childhood when she had been under the rule of her fanatically religious mother, red-haired Morag Ruadh, who hadn't so much played the kirk organ as attacked it and who had almost broken Ruth's spirit with her warped and sanctimonious outlook on life. Somehow, Ruth had emerged from those years virtually unscathed, though there were times when she could be strange and unforgiving and very unyielding. That time with Lorn, for instance, she had very nearly broken his heart by taking Lorna away with her . . . Yet who could really blame her: it had been a terrible time and she, Rachel, had been the cause of it all . . . She shuddered and turned her mind away from such dark thoughts and forced herself to talk of lighter matters. It was like old times – as the young women talked and laughed, Rachel visibly relaxed and forgot herself. She was an island girl again, carefree, abandoned, vowing to herself that as soon as the weather was warm enough she would roam her old haunts, barefoot and free, just as it had been when she was a wild, unsophisticated child with few problems to complicate her life.

Excitedly she recalled those early days, when she and Ruth, Lorn and Lewis McKenzie had wandered the island together.

'Oh, it was good, Ruth,' her fingers formed the words, 'so very, very good. I remember Lewis so well, he was so different from Lorn: he was as devilish and daring as I was myself, as strong as a young horse, while Lorn was quiet and delicate. Oh, how the years have passed – so quickly. Everything has changed: Lewis is dead, Lorn is as strong as his brother used to be. You and I were bound up with the two of them – right from the beginning . . .'

She stared into the fire, her great dark eyes burning as she remembered Lewis. How passionate they had been together in the all-consuming desire of their young love, how much they had hurt one another with their stormy, youthful arguings, how much they had hurt other people . . .

She would never love another as she had loved that wonderful young McKenzie – yet she had left him for Jon because she had always known that there could be no future for her with Lewis, and then he had died and there had been no future for him – with anyone.

Ruth looked at her friend. The firelight was glinting on her raven-black hair; her supple young body, though clad simply in a red jersey and blue jeans, still conveyed that air of erotic sensuality that drew men to her like a magnet. She looked still and composed by the fire, but Ruth knew that beneath the calm exterior she burned with thoughts of two young men, Lewis and Lorn, the twin sons of McKenzie o' the Glen, both of whom had been captivated by her in their turn . . .

Ruth lay back in her seat and she too remembered Lewis McKenzie and how the course of her life had been changed by him during those sad, terrible days when he had told her he was dying. By then, Rachel had left the island with Jon, and in his fear and loneliness Lewis had turned to Ruth for comfort. Lewis had died but his seed had lived on in his daughter, Lorna McKenzie, now nearly six years old. Lorn had married Ruth to give the child his name even though he had at first been devastated to discover that the girl he loved was carrying his brother's child.

Lorn . . . darling Lorn. Ruth had nearly lost him too but in quite a different way from Lewis. Hurtful memories came flooding back. She glanced at Rachel and resentment burned for a few moments. This black-eyed, passionate creature in whom she had always placed a rather childlike trust had had an affair with Lorn behind her back when she had been ill in hospital. It had been a dreadful time, she and Lorn had almost split up because of it . . .

Ruth gave herself a mental shake: it was all in the past, she mustn't think about it, Rachel had made a mistake, she truly loved Jon and would never do anything to hurt him again . . .

'Lorna is Lewis's child!' Rachel's hands moved swiftly, impatiently, as she made the statement.

Ruth gasped. 'How did you know that?'

'I guessed.' Rachel's hands made a succinct reply.

'But – why did you bring the subject up now? It was so long ago. Lorn accepts Lorna as his daughter, everyone, with the exception of family, thinks she's his child.'

'I was thinking of Lewis, remembering how it was with him, wondering, I suppose, what my life would be like now if I'd had his child.'

'You want a baby very much, don't you, Rachel?' Ruth spoke softly, sympathetically.

'Yes, I do. I can sense Jon's longing to have a child, and, of course, Mamma Jodl never stops hinting that it's all my fault we haven't got children. But . . .' Rachel looked straight at her friend, 'I know for a fact it isn't: I went to see a doctor, several in fact, and they all said the same thing. There is nothing wrong with me, I am fit and well and quite able to conceive.'

'Then – you think – the problem lies with Jon?' Ruth spoke slowly, unwilling to touch on such a sensitive subject, even though she sensed that Rachel needed someone to confide in. She had always been deep, had Rachel, fathomless some said. She had never spoken to her mother about things nearest her heart, Jon's mother was as close to her as the man on the moon and she obviously didn't feel able to discuss the matter with her husband, which left Ruth, to whom she had always disclosed her innermost thoughts

'I'm not absolutely sure if there really is a problem,' Rachel replied morosely. 'Our lifestyle isn't exactly a restful one, we have never been able to relax properly and give ourselves up fully to one another. We never have the time, always there are matters more pressing than our private life together. I haven't told Jon that I saw those doctors, I'll wait awhile yet.

'We have the summer ahead of us, possibly the autumn as well, we are both going to take time off and have a long, long holiday together. He'll come home to Rhanna after his visit to Mamma Jodl in Hamburg; we'll have time for one another again, all the time in the world. Who knows what will happen.'

Ruth's eyes were sparkling at the idea of having Rachel on Rhanna for a whole summer. 'Och, Rachel, that's wonderful!' she cried. 'I forgive you for not letting me know you were coming home. It's going to be a wonderful summer, I know you'll want to spend a lot o' your time with Jon, but I also know you'll spare some for me. Kate will be delighted, she aye loves it when you're home and she can show off her famous granddaughter to her cronies. Oh, look at the time! I must fly. Lorna will be home from school soon and I've still to feed the hens and get some messages from Merry Mary's, also I need some things from the Post Office.'

Rachel smiled as she followed her friend to the door. Douglas ran on ahead, eager to be off; one small adventure was over with, now he was impatient to see his sister and tell her all about the pictures he had coloured in that afternoon.

Rachel and Ruth stood for a moment at the door of An Cala. The gorse bushes were coming into flower, the sweet perfume was already invading the air, the Highland cows were browsing amongst the little sheltered hillocks, a nearby burn foamed over a tumble of stones on its way to the sea. How peaceful it was, Rachel thought happily, it was going to be lovely spending the coming months on Rhanna, everything slow-paced and tranquil, no need to hurry anywhere, no noise, no bustle.

Far below, the steamer hove into view. With mild interest both girls watched it sailing past Mara Òran Bay on its way to the harbour.

'The tourist season will be starting soon,' Rachel observed.

'Ay, it has already,' Ruth nodded.

'We'll have strangers on the island,' Rachel continued, a frown on her brow.

'Ach, don't fret,' laughed Ruth. 'They won't intrude on you or Jon. Whatever else the islanders might be, they're loyal to their own and won't tell anyone you're here. They're quite protective of their famous violinist.'

She waved and hurried down the path to catch up with her son. Rachel remained at the door, watching the steamer, and a strange sense of apprehension shivered through her, even though the sun broke warmly through a bank of cumulus that had covered it for the last hour.

Chapter Two

Doctor Megan Jenkins brought her little red Mini to a spectacular halt at the harbour, though her somewhat unreliable brakes were only partially responsible for the sudden stop. A pile of Ranald's lobster pots absorbed the rest of the momentum she had gathered on her rush down the Glen Fallan road and she tumbled out of the car, her hair in disarray, her face red with anxiety.

'You'll do yourself an injury, Doctor Megan,' observed Erchy the Post, keeping one eye on the steamer as she tied up in the harbour. 'If it's the boat you think you've missed you needny worry your head, she's just come in this very minute.'

'Thank heaven for that,' Megan said a trifle breathlessly. 'I was visiting Murdy when I looked from the window and saw the boat heading round the bay. I'm afraid I left poor Murdy half dressed with a thermometer sticking into his armpit and my stethoscope in a heap on top of his chest.'

Erchy grinned and scratched his balding head. 'Ach, he'll have a wee play wi' it while he's waiting for you to come back. Murdy was aye fascinated wi' tubes of all sorts. The inner tubes o' that old bike o' his are more often out than in and I mind once, when Auld Biddy had to give him an enema, he was that taken up wi' all the wee tubes it was all she could do to make him leave them alone so that she could do what had to be done wi' them. Now, any normal body would be fair affronted at the goings-on of enema tubes but not Murdy – oh no – they just gave him an even keener taste for them – if you'll forgive the expression, Doctor.'

He paused cryptically and slid her a sidelong glance but her attention was taken up by the passengers who were starting to come down the gangplank.

'It was a terrible thing, just, what Murdy did to himself the next time he was constipated and needin' Biddy wi' her tubes.'

Erchy spoke heavily and was gratified to see that he had aroused Megan's curiosity. 'Did to himself?' she asked with a faint smile.

'Ay, he thought he knew all about it, having watched Biddy wi' the tubes and the soapy water, so he made his cailleach wash out an old bicycle tube and bring it to the bed along wi' a great bucket o' hot water piled high wi' soap suds. Well, both him and the cailleach between them tried for hours to get things moving wi' the old inner tube. Soap suds were everywhere, on the bed, the floor, even in the cat's ears, everywhere but where they were supposed to go. In the end the pair o' them were that exhausted they fell asleep together in the wet bed. When Biddy heard tell about the affair she was over there like a shot to give them a piece o' her mind. "Is it an elephant you think you are, Murdy McKinnon?" she roared. "I've never heard the likes in all my days as a nurse and it would just have served you right if you had ruptured your bowels and we would all have had some peace without them." ' Erchy shook his head sadly. 'Ay, Biddy was never a one to stand any nonsense from anybody. Never again did Murdy try anything so drastic wi' his inner tubes but it didn't put him off his liking for them – or any tubes for that matter.'

'Quite a story, Erchy,' said Megan drily, though her eyes were twinkling. 'We can only hope he'll be safe with my stethoscope till I go back and rescue it from him.'

'Ach, poor old Murdy.' Erchy's tones were solicitous now. 'I am hoping there is nothing serious wrong wi' him, he never calls a doctor out if he can help it.'

'Just old age, Erchy, and the pains and aches that go with it.'

'Ay, indeed, it must be terrible to be getting old.' Erchy's face was perfectly straight, his words absolutely sincere, for although he was well past retiring age he vowed he would only stop working on the day he dropped dead, and since, in his own mind, such an event was 'years and years away' he went on happily with his work and was as wiry and fit as a man half his age.

'You'll be waiting for someone coming off the boat, then?' Erchy craned his neck and followed the direction of Megan's eyes. Erchy's interest in other people's affairs was legendary.

'No, not quite.' Megan kept her face composed. 'I was wondering, can you see any sign of a flying saucer? I'm expecting one to land at any minute and was told to wave my hanky as a sort of guide.'

'Ach, Doctor!' Erchy scolded huffily. 'There is no need to be sarcastic. I was only making polite conversation. It is the way o' things here, we keep ourselves to ourselves and just get on wi' our own affairs, but it would be unnatural no' to show a wee bit interest in what's going on round about.'

But Megan hadn't heard him. 'Oh, that must be him,' she murmured, her eyes on a tall, masculine figure descending from the boat.

'And who is "him"?' questioned Erchy eagerly, forgetting that he was supposed to be getting on with his own affairs.

Megan didn't answer. Leaving Erchy to observe the bustle of the harbour with avid eyes, she somewhat tentatively approached the stranger who had alighted from the boat and was standing looking around him in a questioning manner.

'You must be Herr Otto Klebb.' Megan extended a friendly hand. 'I'm Mrs James, better known as Doctor Megan – or just plain Megan if you like. My car is just over here, it's very small, I'm afraid . . .' Doubtfully she glanced at his large frame and wondered how such a big man could possibly fit into her small car.

A great stir of interest greeted the newcomer, heads bobbed, a dozen pairs of eyes followed his progress along the harbour.

Herr Klebb was not the usual sort of visitor to alight on Rhanna's shores. He was definitely foreign-looking, which fact alone was enough to rouse curiosity, but there was more to this stranger than just the stamp of a continental. He was a Presence, that was how Robbie Beag put it to Ranald McTavish, who was retrieving his scattered lobster pots with mutters of annoyance.

'A Presence wi' a capital P,' Robbie added. 'He'll be a Somebody, you can aye tell by the look they have on them, as if they owned everything and everybody and expect to get things done for them wi' just the snap o' a finger.'

'Do you suppose Doctor Megan will help me gather up my lobster pots if I snap my fingers at her?' Ranald enquired sourly.

'Ach no.' Robbie's genial face broke into grins. 'She's too busy wi' the foreign gentleman to be bothered wi' you and your pots. You shouldn't leave them lying where folks can crash into them wi' their motor cars – one o' these days someone will break a leg tripping over them and it will serve you right if you get sued for damages.'

Ranald's yelp of indignation was lost on Robbie who had gone to join an inquisitive group all stretching their necks to get a better look at 'the foreign stranger' as he had quickly been labelled.

Robbie, in his own, ingenious way, was right, Herr Otto Klebb was a Presence and a Somebody. Megan sensed these things the moment she had gazed into his piercing, deep eyes. He was at least six feet tall, well built, distinguished-looking despite a mop of dark hair that the sea breeze was blowing into disarray. His black beard was clipped to a neat point, his face was strong and ruggedly handsome but rather severe in its unsmiling repose.

It came to her that she knew very little about the man beyond his name and the fact that he had leased her old home, Tigh na Cladach, for an indefinite period. 'I need a place where I can have complete privacy. I have been working very hard and my doctor has advised me to take a long rest,' he had written in reply to her advert in an English newspaper, 'your house sounds ideal and I will require to move in as soon as possible. Please let me know when it is convenient and also please forward the timetable for steamer connections to Rhanna.'

Megan had married the Reverend Mark James on Christmas Eve just over two months ago and had moved into the Manse, which was a big, old house with enough rooms to allow the two of them to conduct their respective professions comfortably. They had both thought it a good idea to let Tigh na Cladach but hadn't expected that it would be taken quite so quickly.

For some reason Megan felt unnerved by Herr Otto Klebb and she was rather glad when Erchy strolled up to help her lift the man's cases into the boot of the car and to batten down the rusty lid with the aid of an old webbing belt. She immersed herself in the task, not daring to look to see how Herr Klebb was managing to tuck his bulky, overcoated frame into the sagging front passenger seat. But somehow he had made it and, breathing a sigh of relief, she went round to the driver's door.

'He'll be staying at the Manse, then?' Erchy hadn't offered his services for nothing, and he was most annoyed when Megan merely smiled sweetly at him before getting into the little red Mini.

At the first turn of the key, the engine burst into life so vigorously Megan was taken aback. Normally it coughed and died, choked and spluttered, before permitting itself to putter weakly into action, and she was so ridiculously pleased with it, it was all she could do not to laugh outright.

'I hope you don't mind,' hastily she covered the bubbles of laughter in small talk, 'but I have to make a quick stop in Glen Fallan to collect my tubes – er – I mean, my stethoscope. I was out on my rounds when the boat came in and had to leave my last patient in rather a rush. My husband would have collected you but Thunder – that's his car – wouldn't start when we tried it this morning . . .' She paused. She was beginning to sound like an islander and at the very thought of Thunder, with its rattles and draughts, its broken seat springs and disconcerting habit of grinding to a halt in the most awkward places, she felt the laughter rising again. For never, never, could she imagine the dignified figure of Herr Otto Klebb ensconced in Thunder's worn interior, the cracks and crevices of the leather upholstery packed with dog hairs, dusters wedged into the windows to keep out the rain and the wind, the smell of ancient pipe smoke permeating every nook and cranny . . .

'I don't in the least bit mind you going to collect your tubes.'

His voice was deep, soothing, his English perfect with only a slight but pleasing hint of foreign accent. There was no change of expression when he spoke the words but Megan got the distinct impression that he had appreciated her light-hearted chatter and was actually enjoying the experience of motoring through Glen Fallan in a cramped little Mini.

But he said nothing more. His eyes were on the hills, raking the landscape, craning his neck to get a better view of the soaring peaks rising sheer on either side. Floating wraiths of mist curled into the blue corries, the hill burns meandered amongst the hillocks, glinting in the sun as they wound their way in and out, down, down, to splash over boulders and in amongst rocks till finally you could hear the purl and music of them as they fell and tumbled into the River Fallan far below.

Fergus McKenzie of the Glen was striding over the lower slopes of Ben Machrie with Lorn, his son, running along in front, throwing out whistled instructions to a black and white Border Collie who was gathering the hill ewes, bringing them down to the fields in time for lambing.

Dodie, the island eccentric, was making his purposeful way down to the village of Portcull, a tiny white lamb tucked under each arm. Grinning from ear to ear, he was obviously extremely happy, for he normally wore a perpetually mournful expression, and only a chosen few had ever actually heard him laughing aloud, which was as well, because it was a sound that resembled a rusty hacksaw grinding through wood.

Seeing the red Mini, he scrunched to a halt in the middle of the road and, holding up the lambs, he waved them around like little white flags.

'Doctor Megan! Doctor Megan!' he yelled joyfully. 'Look and see what Croynachan is after giving me!'

The old eccentric was either losing his mind altogether or else he placed great trust in Megan's abilities as a driver. For the second time that afternoon and with a muffled curse, she rammed her foot on the brake pedal, an action which caused the car to waltz round in a semi-circle before it came to rest just inches from a ditch.

Furiously she wound down her window and poked her head out.

'Dodie!' she yelled, forgetting Herr Klebb, forgetting everything in her fright and fury. 'What are you thinking of, stopping me like that! I could have killed you!'

Dodie galloped up to gaze at her in some bemusement. An elongated drip adhered to the end of his nose; the large, hairy ears that stuck out from his frayed cloth cap were purple with the cold; his big, callused hands were raw and red in the bite of the wind whistling down through the glen; the threadbare coat that covered his stooped, bony frame would have shamed a tinker and he was altogether inadequately dressed for the breezily fresh March day. The islanders regularly gave him gloves and scarves and other items of warm clothing which delighted him for a time before he mislaid them or lost them or used the coats and jackets as bedcoverings and sometimes even as blankets to tie round his beloved cow, Ealasaid, to keep her warm in her winter byre.

The older he got the more pronounced were his eccentricities, but he was sublimely happy these days, as Scott Balfour, the laird, had recently re-housed him in a sturdy croft cottage on the outskirts of Portcull. There he kept his hens and his cow, tended his flower and vegetable gardens, and was extremely contented with his lot. But the wanderlust was still in him and quite often he took it into his head to roam his old haunts, shanks's pony being the only mode of travel he had ever known and was ever likely to know, for he mistrusted anything on wheels. It was, therefore, all the more surprising that he had forced Megan to stop her car in such a dangerous fashion.

'I could have killed you, Dodie,' she repeated in subdued tones. More shaken than angry now, she was aware of the fact that Herr Otto Klebb was receiving some very peculiar impressions in his first minutes on a remote Hebridean island, even though he said nothing and appeared not to be the least surprised by his informal introduction to a Rhanna native in the somewhat misshapen shape of old Dodie.

'Ach, no, you wouldny do that, Doctor Megan.' Dodie met her words with conviction. ''Tis your place to heal people, no' to kill them.'

'Really?' Megan said faintly.

'Ay, you know that as well as me and I only stopped you because o' these.' Impatiently he indicated the newborn lambs in his arms. 'One o' Croynachan's yowes gave birth to them on the hill and she died even before they could suckle. All the Johnsons but one are in bed wi' the flu, and Archie is too busy to feed these wee lambs. He said I could keep them if they lived and I'm feart they'll die on me if they don't get warmed and fed soon.' Awkwardly he shuffled his large, wellington-clad feet. 'I was wondering, seeing as how you stopped your motor car for me, if you would maybe give me a wee run home in it.'

The enormity of the request appeared to nonplus him for a moment and two spots of red burned brightly in each ruddy, wizened cheek.

Without ado, Megan righted her car and got out to push forward her seat and bundle him into the cramped and congested space at the back. Halfway inside he remembered his manners and gazing at the front-seat passenger with his guileless green eyes he murmured courteously, *'Tha brèeah.'*

In exasperation Megan gave his rickety backside a none too gentle push and without ceremony he collapsed into the back of the car, his long, ungainly legs splayed untidily against the front seats.

'Tha brèeah!' he repeated, breathlessly but stubbornly.

'Yes, indeed.' Herr Klebb felt moved to make some form of reply although he had no earthly idea what the Gaelic salutation conveyed.

'It's Dodie's way of saying "a fine day", Megan explained automatically. 'Rain or shine, the day is fine to Dodie's way of thinking. You'll come across a good deal of Gaelic on Rhanna, the old folk speak it freely while the young ones pretend not to understand even though many of them can converse fluently in both Gaelic and English.'

'And you understand what they're saying?'

'Yes, I knew a bit when I came to Rhanna and I'm learning more and more as time goes by . . . Oh' – her hand flew to her mouth – 'I just remembered . . .'

'You have to call in at some house to collect your tubes.'

Megan glanced at Herr Klebb. His face had remained straight but his eyes were twinkling and she smiled in appreciation of his quick wit. Some of the tension she had felt in his company left her – but there was still that sense of being in a Presence. She was suddenly glad that Dodie was there in the back seat, where the motion of the wheels held him spellbound in a combination of silent fear and fascination, while the waves of unsavoury odours that emanated from his unwashed person let no one forget *his* presence.

'Dodie,' said Megan faintly, 'only last week I gave you a big bar of carbolic soap. Haven't you found a use for it yet?'

Dodie snuggled the lambs closer to his bony bosom, sublimely immune, as he always was, to any innuendo cast at his lack of hygiene. 'Ay, indeed, it was a fine present and just the thing I was needin' for my squeaky door hinges. I just rubbed it all over them and they have never given me any bother since.'

Megan gave up; she put her foot on the accelerator and the little red Mini fairly hurtled along to Murdy's house where she hastily collected her 'tubes' before depositing Dodie at the gate of Croft Beag inside whose portals half a dozen cockerels crowed and strutted and generally created bedlam in the once peaceful village outskirts.

A white net curtain fluttered in the window of Wullie McKinnon's croft which was situated close to that of Dodie's. A cacophony of cockerel voices blasted the air. Wullie appeared at his door, shaking his fist in the direction of Croft Beag. An oblivious Dodie disappeared into his house, intent only on tending his newborn lambs.

'The noise of these creatures drives that gentleman crazy,' observed Herr Klebb unsmilingly.

Megan did smile, but only at the idea of rough and ready Wullie McKinnon being referred to as a gentleman. With few exceptions, that particular McKinnon family were renowned for their blunt tongues and vigorous approach to life's situations, and Wullie had been endowed with his fair share of the family traits.

But Megan didn't enlarge on the subject, it would never do to divulge too many of the islanders' little foibles to a newcomer. Until she knew a little more about Herr Otto Klebb, he was very decidedly a stranger on Rhanna, and with his dour demeanour and withdrawn manner she had the feeling that he would most likely remain so throughout his stay on the island.

Chapter Three

Erchy came puffing into the Post Office with the mail, which he dumped unceremoniously behind the counter, much to Totie's annoyance for, no matter how often she told him not to, he always placed the bulky sacks where she would be most likely to trip over them.

'Erchy,' she said sternly, 'how many times do I have to tell you about these sacks? Only the other day I nearly broke my toe on them.'

He paid no heed, instead he ran his fingers through his sparse sandy hair in a characteristic gesture and intoned importantly, 'A stranger has arrived on Rhanna, he came on the boat and went away in Doctor Megan's motor car.'

'Strangers on Rhanna are nothing new,' Totie snorted sarcastically. 'They come and they go, just like the tide.'

'But this one really is a stranger,' Erchy insisted enigmatically, 'and forbye that he is foreign. You can aye tell the foreigners: they stand outside o' themselves – like ghosts.'

'Here, I saw him too.' Todd the Shod, the island blacksmith, was licking stamps with gusto and slapping them on the letters that his wife Mollie had instructed him to post. 'A big chiel wi' a beard and queer, staring eyes that fair gave a body the creeps. He threw me a look that would have withered a rose when I accidentally knocked against him as he was walking to the doctor's motor car.'

'I noticed the man as well,' volunteered Donald, the young grieve of Laigmhor. 'Fergus asked me to go down to the pier to collect some new calves and I saw this stranger coming down the plank. I noticed him because o' his coat, it had curly grey collars on it and there was money stamped all over him.'

For a few moments Totie digested the various pieces of information before saying heavily, 'Erchy, I shouldn't ask because I know fine I'll get a daft answer, but what similarity is there between ghosts and foreigners?'

'Och, Totie, surely you know that.' Erchy sounded surprised at her obtuseness. ''Tis aye the way o' it, they look as if one half o' them is all dour and disinterested while the other half is watching and observing everything that is going on.'

The doorbell jangled to admit Behag Beag, the Ex-Postmistress of Portcull, as she liked to call herself. When she introduced herself as such to tourists she made it sound like an honorary title endowed with capital letters, for that was how she saw it in her own mind. In she briskly came to dump her message bag on the counter and ask for a packet of envelopes, her quick, beady eyes darting suspiciously hither and thither before coming disdainfully to rest on the arrangement of Post Office material on the counter.

Totie was convinced that the old woman only deigned to enter the premises in order to silently criticise and as a result Totie was always on her guard where Behag was concerned.

'We have a stranger – a stranger on Rhanna,' Behag announced to no one in particular, the pendulous folds of her wizened jowls fairly quivering with each movement of her palsied head. 'I saw him, wi' my very own een, getting into the doctor's motor and driving away in the direction o' Glen Fallan.'

'Ach, that was only to collect her tubes,' Erchy put in knowingly. 'She left them wi' Murdy and God only knows what he did wi' them while she was away at the pier.'

Totie ignored this and leaned her arms comfortably on the counter, an action which incited tight-lipped disapproval in Behag, as never, never, in all her years as Postmistress of Portcull, had she ever allowed herself such levity from the business side of the establishment.

'Fancy, a stranger,' Totie said sweetly, 'getting into the doctor's car – you'll be telling us next that he threw his arms around her and kissed her in full view o' the village.'

'Mrs Donaldson!' an outraged Behag protested.'There is no need to go that far! The man only got into her motor car and never put a finger on her – as far as I could see.'

'He's a foreigner,' Erchy emphasized cryptically. 'Thon kind o' folk are consumed wi' all sorts o' queer passions. Maybe he did kiss her for all we know – when no one was looking that is,' he quickly added at sight of Totie's somewhat fierce expression.

'Ay, and he's staying at Tigh na Cladach,' Tam McKinnon, coming in at that moment with his son, Wullie, promptly entered into the conversation with all the ease of a born-and-bred islander for whom gossip and speculation were second nature. 'I saw the smoke pouring from the chimney as I was passing and the next minute there was the doctor's motor stoppin' at the gate and this big, hairy chiel getting out.'

'Here – talking o' smoke,' Wullie exclaimed, noisily wiping his nose with the back of one large, red hand, 'last night I was going past An Cala on my bike and though it was dark I was sure I saw the smell o' peat smoke. I had a mind to go and see was there anybody in but there were no lights on, only a soft wee keek o' pale darkness at the window that was likely just the sea reflectin' on the panes. Anyway, Mairi was waitin' wi' my supper and I just went on my way.'

He had added the last part hastily, ashamed to admit that he had been too nervous to investigate the deserted-looking crofthouse sitting lonely and silent on the cliffs above Mara Òran Bay.

'You *saw* the smell o' peat smoke?' Totie repeated with a flaring of her strongly chiselled nostrils. 'Wullie, I know fine you've aye been bothered wi' your nose but surely it's time you saw a doctor about your eyes as well – if only to report that the Lord made a miracle when he made you.'

Wullie looked sheepish. 'Ach, Totie, you know what I mean, it's only my way o' speakin'. But I did smell the smoke, my nose wasny lyin', nor were my eyes – there *was* a keek o' light at the windows.'

35

Behag's head fairly wobbled on her scrawny shoulders and she said in a voice full of meaning, 'A foreign stranger on Rhanna and thon Rachel Jodl back on the island – sneakin' back without a word to anybody. She must meet a lot o' they continental people on her travels. Maybe the pair o' them have arranged to be on the island at the same time and each pretendin' that they don't know the other is there.'

'Och, c'mon now, Behag,' Todd said reasonably, his round, cheery face looking serious for once. 'There is no need to go that far, and it might no' be Rachel that is back, it could just as easily be Jon.'

'No, it will be Rachel,' Behag stated with conviction. 'She aye did behave in a strange sort o' way, I used to get the shivers up my spine when she looked at me wi' thon black, glittering eyes o' hers. There's gypsy blood in her and no mistake, she would put a curse on you as soon as look at you . . .'

Tam glared at her. 'I will be reminding you, Behag, that it is my granddaughter that you are speaking about: a bonny, proud lassie who just happened to be born with powers that only sensitive folks like myself can understand. Not only that, she has a talent on her the likes o' which this island has never known and is never likely to know again. Oh, ay, she might no be able to speak through her mouth but she does it wi' her violin, music that might have been composed in heaven itself, so beautiful is the voice o' it.'

It was a profound speech for good-natured, easy-going Tam; Behag had the grace to look ashamed while everyone else nodded their agreement at his words.

'As for you' – Tam spun round to glower at Wullie – ''tis ashamed I am just that a son o' mine should come into a place like this to spread gossip about his very own niece and with no more than a flimsy bit peat smoke to go on.'

Wullie grew bright red and fiercely wiped away a second drip that had gathered on the end of his nose. 'Ach, Father, I didny mean anything when I said I thought Rachel was home.' He rubbed his fingers into eyes that were somewhat red-rimmed. 'I don't rightly know what I'm thinkin' these days. These cockerels o' Dodie's are drivin' me daft altogether. He just won't shut them in at night and the whole six o' them are blastin' away at all hours o' the morning. I'm useless without my proper sleep and if something isny done soon I swear I'll go in there and shoot the whole buggering lot o' them.'

It was the cue everyone needed to turn the talk away from Rachel and the stranger, even though Totie was bristling at hearing Tam refer to her Post Office as 'a place like this', as if he was talking about a den of darkest iniquity.

With the greatest of enthusiasm everyone began sympathizing with Wullie over the subject of Dodie's cockerels whose loud, raucous crowing echoed through the village from dawn till dusk. Several of Dodie's neighbours were affected by the noise but Wullie and Mairi McKinnon, whose croft was right next to Dodie's, suffered the most. At his previous abode, buried in the hills, the old eccentric had been accustomed to doing as he pleased. Because he could never bring himself to kill anything, his hens had proliferated without bothering anyone, but things were different now that he lived in the village and a state of war existed between Dodie and his nearest neighbours which perplexed both parties a great deal, as hitherto they had enjoyed a friendly relationship.

Behag wasn't particularly interested in the chatter about Dodie's cockerels. Her attention strayed and her inquisitive eyes probed the narrow bit of window space above the fluted, flower-patterned curtain.

Flowers! In the Post Office window. Really! That Totie had no earthly idea of what was right for premises such as these. In her day, good, sensible nets had served their purpose well *and* they had lasted for years. Flowers, indeed, faded ones at that – dingy with dust, cobwebs old and new adhering to the corners – and – was that a clumsily stitched tear carelessly concealed by a glass jar of aniseed balls?

Darting forward to closer examine the window coverings her attention was abruptly diverted by the sight of Elspeth Morrison, the sharp-tongued housekeeper of Slochmhor, and Captain Isaac McIntosh, one time sea skipper, standing close together at the war memorial. It *was* them! As bold as brass the two of them, meeting at their favourite place. The scandal of it, both of them old enough to know better, behaving like two young lovers in full view of the public eye – and doing it beside a monument that deserved only humble homage from respectable citizens.

Behag vacated the Post Office with alacrity. She was most interested in the affairs of Elspeth and Captain Mac these days. For some time now, a rumour had persisted that he was thinking of moving in with Elspeth though 'just as a lodger, of course'.

Behag didn't believe that for a minute. Since the demise of his wife, Captain Mac had been casting his eye over the single women of the district. At first he had shown a keen interest in Aunt Grace, as she was known to everybody, but 'just another Jezebel', as decided by Behag, disapproval tautening her thin lips. Then Grace had surprised everyone by marrying old Joe who had now gone to 'join the mermaids in some far off shore' as Grace romantically put it. It was a well-known fact that Bob the Shepherd had had his eye on Grace for a long time and had been biding his time till the coast was clear, and Behag was shocked at the idea of twice-married Grace contemplating taking the plunge for the third time.

But first and foremost in her mind was 'the affair', as she liked to put it, between Elspeth and Captain Mac, and Behag was agog to know what exactly was going on between the pair. Pretending that she was perusing the uninspiring contents of the Post Office window, she kept her head tucked well down so that Totie wouldn't espy her there and wonder what she was doing.

Although the window was anything but clean – another black mark against Totie – it reflected enough of the village to allow Behag to observe a good deal of what was happening in the immediate vicinity. The crafty old woman often made use of available windows in this way and likened the reflections she saw to 'a night at the picture house after a good day's shopping in town'.

Not that the rigid confines of her life had ever afforded her much access to either, but on one occasion, whilst visiting a sick relative in Oban, she had surreptitiously slipped into a cinema to see *Magnificent Obsession* and to her shame had shed a few tears in the darkened hall. In no way could 'the affair' between Elspeth and Mac be termed a Magnificent Obsession, more like a Shameless Disaster in Behag's mind, and any tears she might shed over them were born of sheer frustration, since not by one word had they given away their plans to anyone. Nevertheless, Behag followed their every move with far more devoted attention than she had ever given to any romantic liaison on a silver screen, and she watched the reflected images with utmost curiosity.

Captain Mac, his white hair and beard combed to watered-down obedience, was standing very close to Elspeth's scrawny figure while they talked animatedly, and Behag fairly itched to know just what they had to say that was so interesting. She wondered if she dare take a walk past the war memorial. Elspeth had a sarcastic tongue in her head and wouldn't think twice about airing her views if she thought for one moment that she was being watched. Behag hesitated while she argued with herself. It was a free country, she had as much right as anyone to visit the memorial and pause for a moment while she remembered the young men of Rhanna who had given their lives in the wars, and – here her eyes gleamed – there was that wee wooden bench set into a niche in the stone so that folk could sit and gaze out to sea while they pondered and prayed and gave thanks for their peace-filled existence.

Also, if she went down the lane between the Post Office and the butcher's shop, she could double back to the war memorial via Todd the Shod's and in that way Elspeth needn't see her at all. She could sit on the bench and listen to her heart's content and no one need be any the wiser.

Quivering with purpose she immediately made tracks for the lane and was so deep in thought she jumped like a scalded cat when a loud, mournful voice suddenly proclaimed, 'Tis yourself, Miss Beag – a fine day, is it not? I just came outside to take a wee breath o' air to myself and feeling all the better for seeing yourself as well.'

Behag came down to earth with a thump, quite literally, twisting her ankle on a cobblestone as she turned too hastily to perceive the bedraggled form of Sandy McKnight leaning against the open side door of his butcher's shop. He was a small, miserable-looking bachelor who devoted himself to making money whilst pretending that he had no interest whatever in the material side of life.

Every Sunday without fail he was there in his place in kirk and though he had only been on the island a short time he was now a church elder, aired his many and forceful opinions at church committee meetings and led collections for the Fabric Fund with much devoted energy. He was also a keen advocate of good against evil and loudly denounced all things corrupt and sinful, including in these the evils of tobacco and spirits. But since the day that Todd the Shod had observed him smoking a pipe behind a rock on the seashore, he could have talked himself blue in the face about his piety for all anyone listened.

Thereafter he had been nicknamed Holy Smoke and whenever he aired his views to the men of the village Tam McKinnon would just smile and say, 'Himself is just fatuous, he opens that big mouth o' his and lets out enough air to fill a set o' bagpipes.'

Tam wasn't really sure what 'fatuous' meant but it sounded good and impressed his cronies who didn't know what it meant either, but they took Tam's word for it and no one else ever said it was out of keeping, not even ninety-seven-year-old Magnus of Croy who knew everything, so it must have been all right.

It was doubtful if Behag knew the meaning of the word either, although she owned a set of leather-bound dictionaries and encyclopedias that were kept well dusted and carefully placed in a prominent position on a shelf – a legacy from a distant aunt who had only ever spoken the Gaelic and who had been as wise as Behag as to their contents. But to Behag, anything that might be construed as insulting to Holy Smoke met with her full approval. Her dislike of the 'butcher man' was legendary, she shuddered every time she looked at his drooping 'bloodhound' eyes and the layers of leathery flesh gathered in folds below his chin. When Tam had remarked innocently enough that Holy Smoke's features very much resembled her own and had gone on to wonder if he was a relative of hers she had nearly had apoplexy and hadn't spoken to Tam for a month.

To make matters worse, Holy Smoke had attached himself firmly to her almost from the first day of his arrival on Rhanna, so that she had to employ every ruse she knew in order to avoid meeting him. Whenever she saw him approaching she would scuttle into a shop doorway or sprachle up a bank to hide in a clump of bushes. If none of these were available she was forced to take refuge in a nearby house and people were growing quite accustomed to having Behag suddenly shoot through their door to stand with her eye to the keyhole, or to rush to the nearest window to peep outside from the safety of the window coverings.

She was therefore all the more incensed to be caught on the hop outside the butcher's premises and it was with extreme annoyance that she glared into his mournful countenance as he rushed forward to place his narrow shoulder under her arm and say in his rather feminine voice, 'There, there, Miss Beag, just you hold on to me and we'll have you inside my shop in no time. Ice! That's what you need for that ankle and there's plenty and enough o' that in my freezer room.'

'Will you let go o' me!' panted Behag, struggling with all the might of her shrunken frame to shake him off. 'I have no need o' your shop or of your ice! Unhand me this meenit, Sandy McKnight! I will no' have the gossiping folk o' this parish bear witness to your intimate handling o' my person.'

But Holy Smoke was having none of her protests and spoke to her in a voice that was oily in its attempts to soothe.

'Ach, c'mon, now, you know well enough you like me, Miss Beag, and it's reciprocal, I assure you. Oh ay, I've seen the way you run and hide from me, it's a wee trick that women have, playing hard to get. I saw it often enough when I worked on the mainland and the island women are no exception. Now, enough o' your struggles, just you lie against me and I'll take care o' you.'

Behag was so aghast at his words that it was all she could do to breathe, let alone struggle, and in a daze of pain and shock she allowed him to half carry her into his shop where he deposited her on a chair near the counter, a bucket of sawdust on one side of her and a string of fat pork sausages dangling down from the wall on the other.

'Wait you there,' he instructed masterfully. 'I'll no' be long wi' the ice.'

'My, my, look what the wind blew in!' Kate McKinnon's loud, cheery voice bounced against Behag's eardrums like a portent of doom. 'And hangin' on to Holy Smoke as if he was the blessed St Micheal himself. Spring must be in the air right enough, Behag, wi' all these wee romances blossoming on all sides o' us. First we have Captain Mac and Elspeth, now it seems we can add our very own Behag and our dear, good butcher to the list. I never thought o' this place as being romantic but you just look the part wi' that string o' sausages draped round your lugs and that bunch o' mealy puddings sitting above your head like a chain o' wee black haloes.'

Behag uttered not a word, instead she sunk into her shrivelled frame like a frightened snail, her lips folded so tightly they were just a thin hard line in her wrinkled face. It was too much! Much too much! First that pious, insincere hypocrite pawing at her person while his ingratiating voice droned in her ears, now, Kate McKinnon of all people, with her sarcastic innuendoes and a tongue that 'ran in front o' her' as Jim Jim so aptly put it. She would waste no time in letting the whole of Rhanna know of the incident and Behag went cold as she imagined just how Kate would set about embroidering the tale. But worse than any of these was the interpretation that Sandy McKnight had put on her avoidance of him.

Her ankle throbbed but not as much as her head and she wished, oh, how she wished, that just for once she had left Captain Mac and Elspeth strictly to their own devices.

Chapter Four

Tigh na Cladach was warm and welcoming: a cheerful fire burned in the grate; the chintz furniture, the well-filled bookcases and the pictures on the walls were homely yet tasteful. A tray set with cups and saucers and a plate heaped with buttered scones sat on a small table near the fire, while the teapot, keeping warm on the hearth, emitted an occasional puff of fragrant steam.

Outside the window the great cliffs of Burg rose sheer out of the sea. Little oncoming wavelets made scallops of creamy foam on the silvery curve of the bay; a row of gulls on the garden wall were squabbling quietly amongst themselves while a group of Atlantic seals had arranged themselves decoratively on an outcrop of black reefs that stuck out from the translucent green shallows to the right of the bay.

Herr Klebb strode over to gaze from the window. He stood there for quite some time before turning back to eye the tea things set by the fire.

'Frau Megan, it is perfect.' His tones were vibrant with satisfaction. 'And I see you have been kind enough to also provide me with tea. You have done me proud and I thank you.'

'It's Tina you should really thank, she lives in the village but comes every day to the Manse to look after me and my husband. When I told her you were coming she and Eve – that's Tina's daughter – set to work on this place. I really had nothing to do with the tea but the islanders are very hospitable and to them nothing else in the world beats a good strong cuppy, especially after a long journey. But I know you drink a good deal of coffee in your country, perhaps you might have preferred . . .'

He held up his hand. 'No, tea is perfect, each time I come

43

to Britain I acquire more and more a taste for it and from all I have heard of Scotland I have the impression it is something of the national drink.'

Megan's hazel eyes sparkled. 'Well, I don't think the menfolk of Rhanna would agree with you there, though they would be polite about it and tell you that it was the second national drink.'

'Ah, yes, I know also about the whisky, I have heard a good many tales about the Scottish islands and the illicit whisky stills. Are there any of these left on Rhanna?'

Megan was rather taken aback, she hadn't expected this dour, reserved Austrian to display such vigorous curiosity about an island he knew nothing of, but his previously withdrawn manner had completely disappeared in the last few minutes.

'Oh, you'll have to ask Tam McKinnon about that,' she said with a faint smile. 'I believe he and his cronies unearthed an old still some years ago. It was during the time of the last war and the adventures they had with it are still talked about at the ceilidhs, though it happened well before my time on the island.'

A spark of great interest shone in his eyes. 'Tam McKinnon – tell me, Frau Megan, are there many McKinnons on Rhanna?'

At that she laughed outright.

'McKinnons, McKinnons everywhere! And if they aren't called McKinnon they're connected with them somehow: cousins, wives, aunts. Oh yes, Herr Klebb, we have McKinnons a-plenty on Rhanna.' She went to the door. 'I'll have to leave you now, but if there's anything you need we're at the Manse up there on the Hillock. Don't hesitate to ask if you want something, and Tina will be back later to make your tea. She's quite willing to cook your meals and clean for you while you're here.'

'That arrangement will suit perfectly.' He nodded. 'Oh, and while I remember, I'm expecting more luggage to arrive within the next few days.' He glanced round the room. 'I hope you don't mind if I shift some things around to accommodate it.'

'Oh – no, of course not.' Megan's mind was boggling as she tried to imagine what he meant but she didn't ask: he was preoccupied with his thoughts, the mask of aloofness had

44

settled once more over his strong features. He was frowning as he eyed the furniture as if he was mentally re-arranging it around the room.

It was then she noticed his hands, strong yet beautifully moulded, the fingers long and supple, the nails short and carefully manicured. In Mark's study there hung a print of the famous 'Praying Hands' by Albrecht Dürer and this stranger's hands reminded her of them.

Quietly she took her leave, mystified and fascinated by the man. Getting into her car she drove quickly to the Manse to run inside and shout for her husband.

'In here.' His deep voice filtered through the door of his study. Her heart accelerated and she was enchanted afresh to be living here in this lovely old house with the Man o' God as he was fondly referred to by his older parishioners.

But the Man o' God was also very much a man of flesh and blood and he had arisen from his desk on hearing her voice and was there to sweep her into his embrace when she came through his door.

'Oh, Mark,' she kissed his nose, 'I've missed you.'

He laughed. 'We saw one another this morning.'

'That was in another life.' She ran her fingers through his dark hair. 'So much has happened since then. I had to rush down Glen Fallan to meet the boat and ruined half of Ranald's lobster pots in the process. After that I almost ran over Dodie on the way back up Glen Fallan to collect my tubes and ended up giving him and two newborn lambs a lift back to Portcull before they died. After that I almost knocked down Elspeth and Captain Mac at the War Memorial, then I passed half the population of Rhanna on my way to Tigh na Cladach. Behag gave me one of her 'Thou art a Jezebel' looks as she scurried by on her way to the Post Office, where, I suspect, the entire population of Portcull are gathered to discuss me and my activities.'

He laughed. 'I take it that, in the midst of all this hectic activity, you made time to collect our man from the boat.'

'Herr Otto Klebb, now there is a mystery man for you. He's

big and hairy and built like a great brown bear, he likes tea rather than coffee and seems to know a great deal about island ways though he claims that this is his first time on Scottish soil. He . . .'

'Come on.' Grinning he took her arm and led her to the window seat, there to clear aside two furry dog bundles that were Muff and Flops respectively. Each warm and sleepy heap groaned at the human intrusion but condescended to make room for master and mistress. 'Now,' Mark put his arm round his wife's shoulder, 'tell me all about it. Head back, chest out, deep breath, begin.'

But Megan was rushing on, a vastly changed Megan from the quiet, rather serious young woman who had come to Rhanna almost three years ago to take Doctor McLachlan's place. With an exaggerated sigh of patient resignation he allowed her to describe her meeting with Herr Klebb and when she finished up by saying, 'and he's very interested in the McKinnons, oh not just the likes of Tam and Kate but all the McKinnons that ever were born', he made a great show of surprise and said, 'Oh well, if he's here to study that particular clan we'd better sell him the house because he might just be here forever – and if Kate hears of his interest he'll never get away anyway, she would talk herself blue in the face about the McKinnons, and these just the ones in her particular family.'

Elspeth Morrison entered her cottage and made haste to put the kettle on the fire. While she waited for it to boil she stood staring into the flames, a spot of red burning high on each cheek. Her gaunt, oddly immobile face, for once burned with a welter of emotions, her eyes were dark with excitement. At last! At last! Captain Mac had decided that, come the summer, he was going to move in with her.

'Only as a lodger, you understand, Elspeth,' he had explained earnestly, burying his jolly red beacon of a nose into the depths of an enormous hanky in order to hide his embarrassment. He had thought long and hard before taking this momentous decision and he was at great pains to try and make Elspeth understand that his affection for her was purely platonic. 'It is an arrangement that will suit us both, I'm sure o' that, we are each o' us alone in the world and it will be fine for us to have one another's company in the dark nights o' winter.'

'Indeed it will, Isaac,' she had intoned primly, 'and there is no need for you to emphasize the fact that you will only be biding wi' me as a lodger. No one could ever take Hector's place in my house, dead or alive, he will aye be my man, you know that as well as I do myself.'

It had taken Captain Mac all his time not to laugh outright at this. In his lifetime, drink-sodden Hector had never known a minute's peace from Elspeth's nagging tongue. Their vigorous arguments had never been anything else but public knowledge, for Elspeth had never made any secret of her matrimonial disputes nor had Hector ever tried to hide the fact that 'the cold sea was a far better place to be than a frozen marriage bed wi' naught but the blankets to keep him warm.'

Perhaps time had softened Elspeth's memories of her empty, childless years as Hector's wife, though it was far more likely that she was doing everything in her power to ease Mac's mind about coming to live with her.

In order to hide his incredulous face Mac had pummelled his nose with alarming energy. 'Indeed, I know fine that you will aye be a one-man woman,' he assured hastily, 'otherwise I would never have suggested moving in with you. But it is an arrangement that will suit us both, you need a man to see to the heavy jobs around the house and I need a woman to darn my socks and cook my meals. You understand, of course, that I was never the sort o' man to bide in one place for any length o' time? The sea will aye be in my blood and I couldny live without my wee trips wi' the fisherlads, also, from time to time, I'll be staying wi' my sister Nellie at her croft on Hanaay.'

'Of course, I understand your life is your own to do as you like with,' Elspeth acquiesced readily. 'We will both be leading our own lives, for I have still my duties to see to at Slochmhor. Och, I know fine that Phebie imagines she can do it all herself but Lachlan needs a body like me about the place. I have had a lifetime o' seeing that he has all his wee comforts to hand and I intend to go on doing that till I drop. Besides, Phebie was never much o' a cook, she aye puts too much baking powder in the scones and too much salt in the soup, and too much salt at Lachlan's age isny a good thing. Oh, ay, you and me will lead our separate lives, Isaac, though you can be assured you will aye have a full belly and a good, dry pair o' socks on your feets. Hector had all o' these things and a bittie more forbye, but he was never the sort o' man to appreciate the kind o' comforts a good wife provided.'

'Ay, ay, good friends sometimes make better companions to one another than a wedded pair,' Mac had stated hastily, growing a bit hot under the collar at the enormity of the step he was taking. When his cronies got wind of it they would think he had taken leave of his senses altogether but he had thought the whole matter out very carefully. After a few days living at Nellie's croft she began to nag him worse than any wife and he was glad to make good his escape back to his relatives on Rhanna. But he was growing tired of all the hopping around and had decided that Elspeth was the better of two evils. She was an excellent cook, she kept a tight ship and he knew she was fond of him in her own queer way. If she too started nagging him he could always escape back to Hanaay for a few days and there was always the fishing trips with the lads to fall back on, nevertheless he was aware of a gnawing sensation of unease deep in his belly which moved him to say rather anxiously, 'You are sure you'll no' regret it, Elspeth, and maybe start being annoyed at me for getting under your feets?'

'Ach, of course not, Isaac,' she had returned coyly. 'You should know better than that.'

'And you'll no be worrying as to what folks might be saying about us? I wouldny like to be doing anything that would tarnish your reputation as the good, upright woman that you are.'

Elspeth had snorted. If only he knew! She was longing to have her reputation tarnished! For too many years she had endured the snide remarks of people like Kate McKinnon regarding her 'dried-up opinions about life'. She had been referred to as 'a spinster woman wearing the mantle of widowhood' and 'an old maid who had tripped over the marriage bed and had completely lost her way in the dark'.

She was fed up to the back teeth with Behag's continual prying and poking into her affairs and it would give her the greatest satisfaction to see the look on the old bitch's face when it became apparent that Captain Mac had moved in with her. It was therefore with the greatest conviction that she told Mac he had no need to worry on that score since 'in the eyes o' the Lord she was doing nothing wrong and to hell with gossips and scandalmongers'.

Elspeth sat back and thought of all this while she sipped her tea. For once she had no idea of any of the latest happenings in the village, so taken up was she with her own thoughts and affairs. For a long time she sat in her chair thinking about her meeting with Captain Mac at the war memorial, then, with an oddly furtive expression on her face, she made her way upstairs to her sparsely furnished bedroom. Almost on tiptoe, as if afraid that something or someone might leap out on her at any moment, she went to her dresser and from a bottom drawer she extracted an untidily wrapped brown paper parcel.

'Will you look after this for me?' Mac had asked her a few days ago on returning from a trip to Oban. 'You mind I told you that my brother's widow lives on Uist. There is a daughter, my niece, a right bonny lass who will be twenty-one in November. Joan, that's my sister-in-law, fair dotes on the girl and is planning a big party for her birthday when it comes. She is already gathering things together and bought this parcel o' stuff when I was wi' her in Oban. She doesny want Katie finding them, for she has a wee habit o' snooping into cupboards if she thinks her mother has been hiding things. They'll be safe wi' you till the time comes.'

Elspeth had agreed to keep the parcel but the moment Mac's back was turned she had decided it would do no harm to 'have a wee keek'.

The contents of the innocuous brown wrappings had taken

her breath away. Out had tumbled several luxuriant garments, including two nightdresses, one a peach satin with furls of snowy white lace trimming the low-cut neck, the other a black silk with red ribbon slotted through the black lace at the neck and tiny red bows decorating the hem.

Elspeth had never seen the likes in all her born days and she had spent some time running her hands over the wondrous material. After that she hadn't been able to stay away from her bedroom and at every opportunity she was up there, sitting on her bed, surrounded by black silk and peach satin, enchanted and mesmerized by such beauty.

It was sinful, of course, what mother in her right mind would buy such things for a young girl? It was just tempting providence, any man would go daft with lust and passion if he got just one keek of them covering a young girl's body. It wasn't decent, it wasn't right, it wasn't proper.

Even so, Elspeth's own eyes gleamed at the very thought of that lovely material touching human flesh and very daringly she had crept guiltily to her room one night, undressed and slipped the peach satin over her head. The touch of it on her body was like slipping into the cool, silken waves of the sea. Not that Elspeth had ever dipped herself in any sea, silken or otherwise, but in her heightened state of awareness she imagined that this was what it must be like. She felt pampered, delicious, almost like a girl again, and when she dared to view herself in the full-length wardrobe mirror she imagined she looked like a young girl again, virginal and untouched. Of course, the candlelight was kind, she wasn't foolish enough not to recognize that and never, never, would she dare to garb herself in such a manner in the unkindly light of day. But for just a few, short, ecstatic moments she was the young Elspeth again, before time and care had withered the flesh on her bones and robbed her face of its youthfulness . . .

A shout from outside had nearly caused her to have a heart attack, and rushing to cover the peach silk with her aged brown cardigan she had peered from her window to see Kirsteen McKenzie standing below with a message from Phebie requesting Elspeth be at Slochmhor early next day as visitors were expected for dinner.

'As if she couldny see to it herself,' Elspeth had muttered, contrarily ignoring the fact that she had, for years, tried to brainwash the McLachlans into believing that she was indispensable.

Now here she was again, surrounded by folds of exquisite nightwear that spilled over the patchwork quilt on her bed, like gleaming jewels that taunted and tormented her. It was while she was standing there that an astounding idea came into her head, one so daring that she pushed it aside with an impatient snort. But it wouldn't go away that easily, drumming at her so insistently she felt weak with the power of it, her shaking legs forcing her to sink down on the edge of the bed where she sat, staring into space, allowing the idea to gel and take shape.

Clasping her hands to her mouth, she began to laugh, a small, breathless laugh born of her own audacity. 'I'll show them,' she whispered. 'That bitch, Behag, I'll give her something to talk about, I'll give them all something to talk about . . .'

A voice from the kitchen brought her back to earth with a start. Was there never any peace on this island? At all hours of the day and night there was always someone interfering with her life. Unwillingly and reverently she put the glamorous garments back into her bottom drawer and went downstairs to find Mollie McDonald in her kitchen.

'There you are,' Mollie said with a frown. 'I was beginning to think that the fairies had spirited you away.' She omitted to add that, in her view and in that of quite a few others, Elspeth had been behaving so strangely of late she might indeed be 'away wi' the fairies', but Mollie was too respectful of the other woman's sharp tongue to risk suggesting anything of that nature.

Instead she plunged into the gossip of the moment, knowing that an interest in other folk's business was Elspeth's main pastime. But when she mentioned the 'foreign stranger' and his supposed link-up with Rachel Jodl of An Cala, she met with only luke-warm enthusiasm.

Somewhat unwillingly, Elspeth went to put the kettle on, not in the least bit concerned about a man who was just another visitor to Rhanna – even if he was a foreigner. As Mollie prattled on, Elspeth listened with only half an ear, her mind too busy with her own affairs to be bothered with those of anyone else.

Chapter Five

Tina turned a hot face from the stove as Otto appeared in the kitchen doorway. 'Och, tis yourself, Mr Klebb,' she beamed, tucking away a wilful strand of flyaway hair, 'frozen and done in by the look o' you. It is far too cold a day to go wandering down by the shore. Away you go ben the room to the fire and I'll bring your dinner through on a tray. It won't be long, I'm just waiting for the bone to go out o' the tatties.'

He looked surprised. 'Bones in the – er – tatties?' he hazarded.

'Ach, it's just our way o' saying the potatoes are still hard in the middle. Now, if you'll excuse me for speaking my mind but I don't like anybody under my feets when I'm in the kitchen, so go you through and have a nice warm to yourself by the fire.'

He seemed glad to do as he was bid and when she eventually appeared with a laden tray it was to find him sprawled in a chair with his eyes shut, a look of exhaustion on his face.

'Ach, there now, you've been taking too much out o' yourself,' Tina told him kindly. 'The island air is something you have to get used to bit by bit, the sea has a rough breath to it and tis no wonder your hands are blue wi' cold, you went out without gloves and no' even as much as a stitch to cover your head.'

As she spoke she was setting his meal down on his lap, her actions languid and unhurried, her voice lilting and calm in his ears. When she uncovered the plate a steamily delicious aroma of steak and kidney pudding assailed his nostrils and suddenly and unexpectedly he felt ravenously hungry.

'There you are now, Mr Klebb,' Tina stood back with a beaming smile and folded her hands across her ample stomach, 'just you enjoy that and I want to see every scrap eaten. Neither me nor my Matthew could ever abide waste o' any sort and don't be giving any to that cat, she has her own food in the kitchen but will try to pretend to you she's wasting away wi' hunger.'

Otto looked at the little grey tabby sitting very erect on the hearthrug staring into the fire with huge green orbs.

She had 'come wi' the house' – at least that was what Eve had told him. On his first morning on Rhanna he had gone to the door and there was the cat waiting to get in. She had stalked past his legs, straight in to the house to sit herself by the fire and look at him as if to say, 'Well, I'm home, how about some breakfast.' He had named her Vienna and in the three days he had been at Tigh na Cladach she had only budged from the house when it was strictly necessary. Now he couldn't imagine his hearth without Vienna sitting on the rug or waiting at the door to meet him when he returned from his lonely walks on the beach.

'She thinks she owns me,' he had told Tina, who had informed him, 'She will certainly never disown you as long as you pamper and fuss over her the way you do. Cats are fly craturs, they know where the monkey sleeps and this one is no exception.'

Otto was quite sure that Vienna had no earthly idea where monkeys slept but suspected that it was just another one of Tina's quaint expressions. He only knew that Vienna had found him and was here at Tigh na Cladach to stay, and the minute Tina's back was turned he slipped the little cat a piece of juicy steak which she carried off to a corner like a prized trophy.

He could hear Tina in the hall, singing in a sweet if slightly tuneless voice as she went about dusting, and he smiled to himself because he had witnessed her methods with a feather duster, flicking it about half-heartedly while she studied things that were of far more interest to her.

She had shown a great deal of enthusiasm for the books that he had brought with him and was particularly taken with a volume of Leo Tolstoy's *War and Peace*. Seeing the look on Otto's face, she had smiled indulgently. 'Ach, I know fine what you're thinking, you are wondering what can an island woman like me know about books like these. But the Scottish people have aye wanted to educate themselves, Mr Klebb. You can go into any Highland home and find similar books on the shelves, and old Magnus of Croy who lives in a thatched cottage has a bookcase filled wi' Shakespeare and Shelley, Burns and Sir Walter Scott, wi' a few volumes o' Chekhov thrown in for good measure.

'He also loves good music and on his old gramophone he plays records o' Beethoven and Schumann and that Austrian chiel, Schubert, I think he said. Magnus himself plays the fiddle and makes up wee songs and in his younger days he also played the accordion, the kettle drums, and the bagpipes.'

'Frau Tina,' Otto had said rather severely, 'you don't have to convince me, I know that the Scots have always educated themselves, they are also explorers and have travelled the world in search of fame and fortune and have sought the knowledge of other cultures, though never do they lose their pride in their Scottish roots – that I know for a fact,' he ended on a somewhat mysterious note.

'You can take *War and Peace* home with you and read it at your leisure,' he had added, and an appeased Tina had gone away clutching the book, thinking to herself that he was a generous man under that stand-offish exterior and that there was also something very odd in the way he spoke about the Scots, almost as if knew them very well or had made it a point to find out as much as he could about them.

Having finished the dusting, Tina returned to the living room to pile more peats on the fire and take Otto's tray from him. 'There now, you enjoyed that,' she said, gratified when she saw the empty plate. 'Visitors always get a good appetite when they come to Rhanna, the fresh air is just the thing many o' them need to get them back on their feets again, but you mustny think you have to go off on your own all the time. It will be nice for you to meet other lads who come from the same country as yourself. Two nice young Germans crash-landed their airyplane on Rhanna during the war and later, one o' them, Anton Büttger, who has a farm above Mara Òran Bay, came to settle here, the other, Jon Jodl, has a house near Anton's and comes to it with his wife whenever they can get away.'

Otto looked at her in some annoyance and said harshly, 'Frau Tina, because you speak English does it follow that you are from England? No, of course it doesn't and the same applies to me, I speak German but I am an Austrian and proud of it.'

Tina had coloured but she was not to be browbeaten. 'And I am a Gael, Herr Klebb, and proud to be such, the Gaelic is my native language but if I had never learned the foreign tongue I would not have been counted. German, Austrian, English, Scottish, we are all alike in the eyes o' God . . .' her dimples showed, 'just as long as we all learn English in order to understand one another!'

He looked at her, she had a nice face, open, honest and kind. Megan had told him all about Tina, how she had lost her husband when he had gone out with the lifeboat during a terrible storm only last spring. The same sea that had taken her husband had also brought with it two young men who had been the cause of a different kind of havoc on the island.

Otto didn't know all the details but he had gathered that Mark James, Megan's husband, had suffered some sort of breakdown as a result of the storm and that Tina's daughter, Eve, had been seduced by one of the young men, resulting in her becoming pregnant, and the baby was due some time this month.

Tina had had more than her share of suffering, yet a smile was never far from her face, a song always ready at her lips, and he felt ashamed for his outburst.

'We understand one another, Frau Tina,' he said gently. 'We are of the same soil, the surge of the western ocean beats as strongly in my heart as it does in yours, the voice of lonely places speaks in my soul as it has done for as long as I can remember.'

The mystery was deepening. Tina opened her mouth to speak but he put a finger to his. 'Hush, *mein Frau*, the time will come but for now I am not yet ready for it. It is enough that I am here, warming myself with spicy-smelling peat fires and finding out for myself the meaning of good, wholesome Scottish cooking, the steak pie was *köstlich* and I am feeling fit to burst. Now, if you will excuse me, I have many things to do and I am sure that you too have much bustle in your life.'

He made a neat little bow and escorted her to the door, there to lift his face appreciatively to the sky and sniff the salt-laden air.

A figure came flying along the road on a bicycle, her black hair streaming out behind her, her long legs pushing the pedals with energy.

A spark of interest showed in Otto's eyes as they followed the progress of the girl on the bike.

'Thon bonny cratur is Rachel Jodl,' Tina explained. 'She is married to Jon, the lad I was telling you about. Rachel is a famous violinist, she has travelled all over the world.'

'But, she is so young.'

'Ay, she is that, but from the start she knew where she was going. We are all very proud o' her.'

'Rachel Jodl,' he repeated thoughtfully. 'I see, and you say she is a famous violinist? Ah, yes, I've heard of her – and she is married to this German you speak of?'

'Ay, our very own Jon Jodl though, of course, she is really a McKinnon whose mother, Annie, is the daughter o' Kate and Tam McKinnon.'

She paused expectantly, Megan having told her about the stranger's interest in that particular clan, but though there was a slight lifting of his brows he said nothing and she went on, 'Jon loved Rachel from the moment he clapped eyes on her going barefoot about the island like a wee gypsy. Och, but it was such a romantic affair between the two,' Tina said dreamily. 'Just like a fairy tale, it was: he waited till she was grown up enough to marry then back he came to Rhanna to carry her off into the big, wide world.'

Otto's eyes twinkled. 'You're sure he didn't magic her away on a pure white charger?'

'Ach no, nothing like that, though mind . . .' Tina looked at him, 'Ach, Mr Klebb, you're no' the big, dour chiel you would have us think. A white charger indeed . . .'

She went off down the road chuckling, leaving Otto to go back indoors with a very pensive expression on his face.

The harbour was a-bustle with movement and noise. The steamer had disgorged its usual cargo of mail and supplies and some of the visitors were making their way to the hotel, though several straggled behind to look in the window of Ranald's craft shop and comment to one another on the price of the displayed goods.

The travelling people had also arrived on the boat and were making great play with their motley collection of dubious-looking possessions, though they weren't too busy to arrange their 'star attraction': a tattered old gnome of an Irishman bearing an accordion as big as himself, in a prominent position close to Ranald's shop. A tiny little dwarf woman with straggly black hair and a great long beanpole of a man arranged themselves on either side of the accordionist, a key was struck and a vigorous rendering of 'Danny Boy' soared aloft, causing the visitors to abandon their interest in Ranald's shop and turn it instead to the musicians.

'Ah, is it not a song to pluck the heartstrings?' inquired a young traveller with broken brown teeth, whose heartstrings were sufficiently intact to enable him to place a smoke-blackened pot at the accordion man's feet. 'And surely worth a few pennies for the honour of listening to music from the fingers of a man just risen from his deathbed. Ah yes, the good Lord Himself had a mind to take Aaron that he might join the heavenly band o' the angels but then He saw fit to spare him so that ordinary mortals like us might have the pleasure of his music.'

The dwarf woman, who went by the appropriate name of Tiny, suffered a fit of coughing at this point while Aaron himself struck two discordant notes in quick succession.

'Aaron, you say?' asked one large woman suspiciously. 'That's a very biblical name for a – er – travelling person.'

'Ah indeed, you are right in what you say, me fine lady,' the broken-toothed youth agreed while he listened with half an ear to the satisfying sound of money chinking into the pot. 'But a good upstanding man like Aaron has every right to the name that his old mother put upon him. His older brother's name was Moses and no woman could have had two finer sons. I never knew old Mo myself but it is said he was the greatest violinist this side o' heaven and played music so fine that even the very seals of the ocean would climb on to the rocks to hear him.'

'And you, young man, what is your name?'

'Nothing fancy at all, me fine missus, just plain Joe – Joe Ford Backaxle if you have a mind to hear my full title and now, if you'll be excusin' me . . .'

Rachel arrived in time to hear old Mo's name and to see the look of bemusement on the woman's face as she stood wondering if she had just had her leg well and truly pulled.

Rachel had come on the sturdy black bike she had hired from Ranald for an indefinite period. Although she had been on Rhanna less than a week, she was already a familiar figure as she flew along the island roads on her bicycle. She had suffered quite a few hints and innuendoes because of the secretive manner of her arrival, but on the whole everyone was pleased to see her back. Even Annie, her mother, who had never quite learned how to handle her beautiful daughter's fame, had greeted her warmly, and, of course, Kate had welcomed her granddaughter with open arms and had sat back to bathe in the reflected glory – 'wearing thon big head she grows whenever Rachel's name is mentioned,' old Sorcha had sniffed, turning down her deaf aid so that she wouldn't have to suffer too much of Kate's prattle.

As for Rachel, she was revelling in the freedom of being back home on Rhanna and had had a wonderful few days exploring all her old haunts and popping in to all the familiar houses to strupak and catch up on island news. She took an absolute delight in visiting Fàilte where the children fussed over her and Lorn and Ruth made time to sit with her and listen to all the exciting tales of her travels.

On hearing that the travellers had arrived, she had fairly whizzed down to the harbour to see them. Her mane of black hair had come loose from its imprisoning red band so that the wind caught it and tossed it hither and thither; her black eyes sparkled in a face that was rosy from the exhilarating ride over the moor road. Though the day was breezily fresh she wore a pair of white shorts that showed off her long shapely legs to perfection and so untamed was the quality of her gypsy-like beauty she might have belonged to the dark-skinned band of travellers themselves.

She was overjoyed to see them again. As a child, running wild and carefree over the bens and glens of Rhanna, she had often gone over to their encampment. There she had been warmly invited to 'come in about'. She had eaten and drunk with them at their smoky campfires, had played with the motley and mangy collection of cats and dogs, and had joined the dusky-skinned children in their games.

It had been her delight to lay down her curly dark head on a pillow of fragrant heather and to gaze up at the sky as she listened to some wise, sad voice recall the old days and the old ways while woody sparks exploded in the fire and a battered tin kettle sang on the hot stones.

Mention of old Mo had brought back a flood of memories. How she had loved that dear old man. He and she had played their fiddles together and it had seemed to her that the very music of heaven itself poured from his nimble fingers. To the beat and hush of the ocean, to the flight of the migrating geese, to great red balls of fire sinking into crimson seas, she and he had played their haunting melodies and she had never minded that he had 'wet his dry thrapple' with the water of life and had often become so inebriated she had had to push him home in his battered old pram and had helped to get him into bed in his tent.

At his request she had played to him when he was dying and from his deathbed he had blessed her with his last breath and had made her take his treasured violin to keep as her very own. Jon had told her it was a Cremonese, made by the great craftsmen of northern Italy, but the value of it hadn't mattered to her, more important to her was the knowledge that her lovable old rogue of an Irishman had entrusted the beautiful instrument to her care and from that day on it had rarely left her keeping.

'You have the touch of the angels in those hands, mavourneen,' the old man had said as he lay peacefully waiting for death to come to him. 'Indeed you have more gifts than you know of yourself – and many of them at your fingertips.'

Over the years his words had come true time after time for, as well as their genius for music, Rachel's hands had healing properties that had become a source of wonder, awe and fear to those who had been touched by her powers. Many mistrusted her because of her strange gifts, others accepted them, one or two who had been directly helped by them regarded her with respect and wouldn't hear a wrong word against her.

Not caring what anyone thought, she had gone off with Jon into a daunting world of music. Though young, inexperienced and often afraid, she always had Jon to turn to when the going got hard, and when he wasn't there she had old Mo's violin to see her through her lonely hours. On it she had played her finest pieces and had composed violin solos that had been hailed and recognized throughout the land. Whenever she placed it under her chin she remembered old Mo and in her heart she was certain that he was up there on the concert platform with her, guiding the bow, touching the strings along with her.

It had been a long time since she had met with any of the travellers; many of the children were new to her and stared at her with sullen eyes, while a big rough-looking man standing a little way off was watching her with brooding black brows, but the rest greeted her as if they had parted just yesterday, without fuss or embarrassment, though each and every one of them knew of her fame.

'It is yourself, mavourneen!' Tiny cried, her small Irish pixie of a face creasing into smiles of welcome. 'Bejabers and bejasus! And lookin' as fit and as bonny as the bluebells in May.'

Long ago, and to herself, Rachel had christened the dwarf woman 'Little Lady Leprechaun' because of her size and her habit of garbing herself in green, and laughing she took the tiny hands in hers and spun Lady Leprechaun round and round till they were both dizzy and breathless.

'Indeed, Miss Rachel, it is a sight you are for sore eyes!' exclaimed an odoriferous man known appropriately as Stink the Tink. 'Will you be coming in about when we have settled ourselves at the camp?'

The travellers had long ago learned to understand her sign language, but all she needed then was a nod and a smile to let them know that she would indeed be over to see them as soon as she could.

At that moment a ramshackle lorry appeared round the side of the craft shop. From it descended Ranald, who absorbed the scene in one glance, his face thunderous when he saw that the travellers were taking all the attention away from his carefully arranged window display.

'Get away from there!' he ordered The Beanpole, the idea that he might be losing trade putting a harsh note in his tone and emphasizing the 'wee bit twist to his face'. 'And don't any o' you be going round the back o' my premises to use my wall as a lavatory. If it's no' dogs and towrists it's tinks and the sooner the council do something about it the better I'll be pleased!'

Chapter Six

Behag was sitting on a kitchen chair outside her cottage, her 'spyglasses' to her eyes as she avidly watched all the activity at the harbour from the privacy of her tiny garden with its encircling wall. Her twisted ankle was swathed in bandages and she had endured a very frustrating time of it since her accident. Much to her horror, Holy Smoke had called in to see her every evening after he had shut up shop, and the agony of not being able to escape those visits had been almost too much for her to bear.

He had blamed himself for her mishap and in an attempt to pour oil on troubled waters his manner had been a combination of mournful concern and useless advice as to how best she could mobilize herself till her ankle was healed. He offered to bring in her fuel from the fuel shed, he suggested fetching her pension from the Post Office, he said he would do her shopping for her and even help her along to the kirk on the Sabbath by means of an ancient wheelchair that old Meggie of Nigg had demoted to the junk shed.

During the utterance of this last suggestion he was gazing hopefully at the ancient besom reposing in a corner, as if that too might be employed to whisk Behag around the island. A vision of her astride the broomstick, her straggly hair flying out behind her as she sailed in front of a full moon, haughtily giving that royal wave of hers, popped suddenly into his mind, and, for once, he nearly forgot to keep a straight face.

But this was Behag, a very thunderous-looking Behag, with the folds of skin at her jowls sagging further and further into her scraggy neck as she listened to him in the sort of silence that her brother Robbie had once described as 'shoutin' aloud wi' her accusations'.

So Holy Smoke wisely composed his countenance into its usual expression of doom and carried on listing all the things he felt he could do to make the old woman's life bearable. He offered her just about everything under the sun and when, eventually, he came to a halt he was breathless and bloated with his own magnanimity, but still found the strength to bow his head, clasp his hands to his perpetually downcast mouth and murmur a few words of prayer to the Almighty.

Behag sat ramrod straight, utterly disgusted by 'all the bowing and scraping' and the empty promises. But then she asked herself, were they empty? The man seemed positively to be tripping over himself to please her and – was there more than just a touch of fear in his attitude towards her?

A suspicion grew in her mind: she had seen that self-same look on another occasion, when she had been in charge of the Post Office and he had come creeping in to deeve her with a whole list of sorrows and worries that had turned out to be a preliminary to his having to part with more money than he liked.

She looked at her ankle reposing on a rafia stool in front of her. It had something to do with that, and she searched her mind, going back to the time when she had stumbled over some of the junk he had left at his side door . . .

Behag drew in her breath. So, that was it! She had injured herself because of his carelessness and he was terrified that she might think to sue him for it. She hugged herself with glee; a feeling of power possessed her, making her puff out her bony chest and smile to herself with utter satisfaction. She would make him pay all right. By the time she was done with him she would have him where she wanted him – right in the grip of her all-powerful palm.

Settling her tweed skirt demurely round her legs she cleared her throat and said, 'Well, Mr McKnight, I can see only too well how anxious you are to please me. You can just forget about all these other things, Isabel and Mollie between them have promised to see to my messages and my pension and anything else I'll be needin' while I am laid up.' She cast down her eyes. 'When Nurse Babbie was in seein' to my ankle she was just after sayin' how thin I was and how I should be buildin' myself up wi' some good cuts o' red meat. Seeing as how you're so eager to help, you will no' be mindin' if I ask you to bring a pound or two o' your best steak next time you come. By that time I will have decided what else I need to keep up my strength, at my age my bones are no' as supple as they were and as my very own mother aye said, "Old bones need good feedin' if they are to carry a body through the evenin' o' their days", and though I was too young at the time to see the sense in what she meant I know well enough now but was never able to follow her adage wi' just my pension to keep me going.'

Holy Smoke was flabbergasted, his entire countenance nose-dived to his knees and he stared at her as if she had just taken leave of her senses.

'Ach, come now, Miss Beag,' he cajoled weakly, 'there is no need to go that far. If I was to hand out meat to every pensioner on Rhanna I would go out o' business. As it is I have a hard job to make ends meet and . . .'

'Best steak or nothing, Mr McKnight,' Behag intoned firmly. 'Of course, if you prefer to compensate me wi' sillar instead I will have no objections, though, of course, it would have to be done through all the proper channels.'

The butcher opened his mouth, shut it, opened it again. Like a fish out o' water, Behag thought, hugging herself at his reactions to her 'wheeling and dealing' – she had read that in a magazine and was delighted to be able to apply it to a situation of her very own.

It's blackmail! Holy Smoke decided to himself. Blatant, heartless blackmail! And to a Christian man like me who wants only to do good to my fellow men – and women!

He stuttered, he protested, he listed a whole catalogue of financial worries that kept him from his sleep at night, but Behag, firm, calm, and unflustered, was impervious to all his pleadings.

In the days that followed he appeared regularly at her

door bearing parcels of meat and poultry. Behag had never eaten so well for years and was even able to withstand Kate McKinnon's sly remarks and innuendoes concerning the butcher man's visits.

So all in all Behag was right pleased with herself and was even beginning to enjoy her invalid status. As well as all the goings-on in the village and at the harbour, she was able, with the aid of her spyglasses, to watch what went on at Elspeth's house, though she was rather annoyed that Jim Jim's gable wall restricted some of her view. Nevertheless she could see enough to satisfy her, but had been disappointed so far in that very little of interest was happening in that quarter. But it would come, she was certain of that; meanwhile there was plenty and enough to occupy her. Today it was the harbour and the tinks and 'that Rachel' cavorting amongst them as if she was one of them – though that wouldn't surprise her as God alone knew what kind of mischief the girl's mother had gotten up to in her younger days.

She panned the village, pausing again at the harbour. Wait now! Something else was happening down there. That strange foreign man had arrived and there was a lot of activity on the pier. What on earth was that swinging on the end of the ship's crane? A crate of some sort! Now, what was in it and who was it for . . . ?

There was indeed a great stir of excitement at the pier. First Otto Klebb had arrived in the minister's motor car. Mark drew Thunder to a squealing halt and felt quite gratified that the engine kept ticking over after he had removed his foot from the accelerator.

'Are you sure you don't want me to stay and help?' he enquired of his passenger, but Otto shook his head and gave a wry little smile.

'You are very kind to ask but the village stalwarts were very keen to offer their services when they heard that I was expecting an important shipment to come off the boat. It was good of you to bring me down in your car, I could easily have walked.'

Mark threw back his dark head and laughed. 'You're too

66

polite, Otto. After a run in poor old Thunder most people tell me they wished to God they had walked! It is an experience that takes a bit o' getting used to but never mind, you're here, and I will bid you good day and good luck getting Tam and the others back up to your house.'

'But, it is they who are taking me back to the house to help me unload the lorry.'

Mark grinned. 'It is well seeing you're new here, Otto, but you'll learn, you'll have to if you're to survive living on Rhanna.'

With a cheery wave he revved up and rattled away, leaving Otto to make his way down to the crowd that had gathered on the pier to watch proceedings. On the way Otto passed Rachel. Briefly their eyes met and held; awareness sprang between them. It was her first encounter with the man whose name had touched many pairs of lips since his arrival. Those black, intense eyes of his were compelling in their power. Her heart beat a little faster. So, this was 'The Stranger', this big bear of a man with his distinguished demeanour that suggested great strength of character and a magnetic personality. He gave the distinct impression of one who was used to having his commands obeyed and from all she had heard of him he had already gained a reputation on that score by sending everyone scurrying to obey his will 'wi' just the snap o' a finger'.

Executing a polite little bow he dismissed himself and she watched him walk away, something telling her that her stay on Rhanna was to be one that she wouldn't forget in a hurry. The thought brought that strange little shiver to her spine again and she couldn't tell if it was one of apprehension – or anticipation.

The sight of the enormous crate swinging on the end of the crane had brought forth much speculation from the onlookers.

'It could be a bed,' hazarded Graeme Donald, who had abandoned his net-mending in favour of the latest diversion. 'Folk can be very queer about beds and like to sleep on their own instead o' one that dozens o' people might have used.'

67

Fingal McLeod agreed thoughtfully. 'Ay, people do some terrible things in bed. I wouldny like to sleep on one that wasny my own in case somebody else had done worse things on it than I had done myself.'

'A bed that size!' Todd the Shod expostulated. 'No, no, it canny be a bed – unless Mr Klebb is planning to ship over an elephant to sleep on it.'

'Here, maybe he is Count Dracula in disguise,' suggested Ranald, who, as well as being a keen reader of mystery and adventure stories was also a devotee of horror films and went to see as many as he could when he had reason to visit the mainland. 'I saw a picture once where Dracula shipped himself over the sea in a coffin which was stored in the hold. His henchman kept a tight watch on him and made sure his master was always back in his coffin before sun-up.'

Ranald's eyes gleamed. 'It was terrible just, by the time the boat touched dry land he had drunk gallons o' blood. Half the folk were dead or dyin' and a whole new batch o' vampires were busy sharpening their fangs ready to do business the minute they went ashore.'

'Ach, you and your horror stories!' Captain Mac said scathingly. 'How can Mr Klebb be a vampire when he walks the daytime hours the same as the rest o' us . . . ?'

The arrival of Otto on the scene effectively quelled further comment. Tam too arrived, looking puffed and important, for had not the 'stranger mannie' more or less implied that he was to direct proceedings that day? Tam was full of himself, though he was also rather peeved that he hadn't been told just what it was that was arriving on the boat.

'All in good time, Herr Tam,' was all Otto would say, and Tam would have argued further if he hadn't been so tickled at being referred to as 'Herr Tam', which to his ears sounded very much like an honorary title.

Aaron was leaning against Ranald's boatshed while he watched proceedings from a safe distance. Aaron had always watched anything of an energetic nature from a safe distance ever since he had been called to help with a flitting which he claimed had racked his back so badly it was a wonder he hadn't landed up an invalid for the rest of his days. Not that that would have worried him greatly. Mo, his brother, had spent his latter years being pushed around in a huge baby carriage, his excuse being that his legs were incapable of carrying him, and there might have been some truth in that since he was 'legless wi' the drink' half the time and the other half he passed sleeping off his excesses.

It was a blue, blue afternoon; the sea was aquamarine, the sky azure, and the two met and married in a tranquil celebration of coming spring. Thus thought Aaron in his rather poetic way. He liked poetry, did Aaron, he liked to read it and listen to it and sometimes he enjoyed making up little verses when he felt the inclination to do so.

He liked Rhanna; it was good to be back on the island with all the long days of summer ahead.

His glance fell on Rachel who was on the fringe of the crowd looking on, an onlooker like himself, never quite belonging but seeing more and hearing more because of it. Creative people like him and her were like that, they had to stand back in order to see everything from a wider angle than mere ordinary mortals. He was glad that Mo had given her his violin, Aaron had never grudged her that though he knew for a fact that a few of the others had, in particular, Paddy, whose resentment over the affair had been simmering for years.

Aaron's languid gaze shifted to Paddy who was sitting on a rock idly playing with pebbles. Aaron sighed, he hoped there wouldn't be any trouble with Paddy that summer. Paddy somehow always managed to make trouble and the other travellers were kept on their mettle whenever it looked as if something was brewing in his mind.

Ranald was backing the lorry as far down to the landing pier as he dared. There was much loud shouting and instructions. The big foreign-looking man was in the midst of it all, giving out orders which everyone seemed only too eager to obey.

Feeling safe amidst all the diversions, with everyone's attention centred on loading the crate on to the lorry, Aaron slunk to the back of Ranald's boatshed to relieve himself against the wall.

'My, my, would you look at that now,' observed Hector the Boat who was diligently if messily slapping tar on the upturned bottom of a big clinker dinghy. 'That shed will be floatin' away if he's no careful and one o' they days its founds will be that rotten it will come crashin' down about Ranald's ears. I'm surprised it's lasted so long, for if it's no' dogs peein' against it, it's some dirty old bugger who hasny the decency to use the bushes like every other body.'

'Ay, ay, terrible just,' agreed Jim Jim, who was bothered with a weak bladder and who had, on countless occasions, been one of the 'dirty old buggers' as well as watering just about every bush and tree this side of the island.

Aaron was barely halfway through his ablutions when he was joined by two small boys who, without preliminary, solemnly undid their trousers to add their contributions to the wall.

The large visitor lady, not in the least interested in the arrival of the crate but totally fascinated by the tinkers despite having been taken in by them, had, after a minute or two of indecision, made up her mind to follow Aaron to see what he was about.

When she saw the trio of masculine figures rowed against the wall, letting off steam as it were, her face was a picture of shocked surprise.

'Really!' she exclaimed forcibly. 'How utterly disgusting! There are places for that sort of thing, but then I expect people like you must be used to behaving like animals!'

Aaron, his back bristling with embarrassment, remained rigidly facing the wall, but his young confederates had no such reservations. With mischievous grins splitting their merry faces they turned round to vigorously shake their small appendages at the aghast lady.

Her face crimson with outrage, she made a hasty exit from the scene much to the boys' disappointment as they had been hoping to squeeze some more fun from the incident.

Jim Jim and Hector roared with laughter. ''Tis a miracle she saw them at all for all the stoor and the steam,' Hector said in delight.

'Ay,' Jim Jim agreed, 'and if the poor wifie but knew it, she herself might be forced to behave like the animals when she realizes there is no proper water hole at the pier or anywhere else for that matter. The council lads on the mainland are in no hurry to build a wee hoosie and it might be years before they make up their minds.'

Hector grinned. 'And by that time, Ranald's shed and all who sail in her might just break from her moorings and slip into the sea leaving no survivors.'

Chapter Seven

Otto was beginning to realize what Mark had meant when he wished him luck getting home. Just when it seemed the lorry was at last about to move off, Ranald glanced in his wing mirror and what he saw there made him jump yelling from the cab to chase after Aaron who, disliking trouble as much as he disliked work, took to his heels and went pelting energetically in the direction of Glen Fallan.

'Come back!' Ranald roared, standing in the middle of the road and shaking his fist at the disappearing Aaron. 'I know what you were up to! You were fouling my premises again. If I catch you at it once more I'll have the law on you, that I will!'

Since the law was safely ensconced several miles over the ocean in Stornoway, Aaron knew well enough that it was an empty threat, even so he had had experience of Ranald McTavish's temper and he kept on running till he had put a good half-mile between himself and the village. Feeling very hard done by he sunk himself on to a heathery knoll, there to regain his breath and wait for the rest of his band to catch up with him.

'My good man, you have my sympathies,' the large lady visitor threw at Ranald as she passed by. 'Why these people can't use the public conveniences like everyone else is beyond me but as I have already said, they have no shame or any sense of self-respect at all.'

'Public conveniences?' Ranald stared at her in surprise then glanced behind him as if to ascertain for himself that a public toilet hadn't miraculously sprung up on the pier. 'Towrists – mad

– the lot o' them,' he muttered, before going back to the lorry to vigorously kick it into life once more.

Four men were perched on the back of the lorry, one more was in the cab beside Ranald and Otto. Tigh na Cladach was reached without further interruption; at the gate two more of the village men were waiting to help with the unloading and Otto breathed a sigh of relief when at last the crate was sitting at the gate ready to be unpacked.

Armed with jemmies and hammers, the men set to with a will, for it could be safely said that each and every one of them was agog to see what would finally be revealed. The metal bands that held the wood fell away, then the wooden slats themselves were removed and finally, with many warnings from Otto ringing in their ears, the men peeled away layers of packing and padding.

At last, at last, it stood there in all its naked glory, a Bechstein baby grand piano, its rich dark wood gleaming in the sun.

'My, my, she is beautiful just.' Reverently Tam removed his cap, as if he was in the presence of some grand lady.

'Ay, a fine piece o' workmanship indeed,' added Ranald, who had, all of his days, loved working with wood and enjoyed the challenge of restoring battered sea vessels to something of their former glory.

Wullie looked at the piano then at the house. 'She'll no' go in there,' he stated with conviction. 'Yon doors are narrow and there's that funny wee bit turn as you go from the lobby ben the room.'

'She will go in.' Otto was already, and quite unconsciously, adopting the islanders' habit of bestowing male and female genders on all sorts of inanimate objects. 'Myself, I have measured and made certain before sending for my piano. It is a big enough house, the doors are good and wide: up on her end in a very undignified fashion, my Becky will go in. One inch, two inches at a time, you will carry her and I will be here guiding you every footstep of the journey. Wullie, will you be so good as to hold her here and you, *Herr* Tam, be so kind as to come to this end. Gently, gently now, Becky is very precious to me and I will not like it if there is one single scratch on her when finally she is settled.'

'*Herr* Tam', beaming from ear to ear at being singled out as the leader, went willingly to do as he was bid but the smiles soon left him during the marathon task of getting the piano through the narrow gate and up the path to the house.

Vienna came out to sit on the step and daintily wash her white bib before settling back to view proceedings in a very statuesque manner.

Bit by bit, little by little, the procession made its slow and painful way up to the house. The men sweated and puffed, they cursed and they groaned and all the while Otto hovered, making sure that not one single mark broke the perfect skin of his beloved baby.

At one point he even took out his hanky to flick away a speck of dust and accidentally gave 'Herr Tam's' nose a wipe in the process.

After the door had been negotiated with great difficulty and the men had paused to gulp in air, Wullie was rash enough to lean his arms on 'Becky' and brought upon himself a sharp rebuke from her owner.

Otto had already enlisted the services of Mark and Megan to help him clear a space over by the back window of the sitting room which looked out to the sea and the sands and the great bastion of Burg rising sheer out of the ocean, a view which never ceased to enchant the new resident of Tigh na Cladach.

On this spot Becky at last came to rest and with one accord the men gave vent to rasping gasps of relief now that the ordeal was over.

Vienna, her tail waving in the air, came over to sniff and examine the latest addition to the household. Otto threw her an indulgent smile, his dark eyes snapping as if at some private joke.

'The little cat, she is thirsty,' he told the men, 'and you, you must also be ready for something to drink.'

Again Tam removed his cap, this time to scratch the sweaty red band it had left on his forehead. 'That is indeed kind o' you, Mr Klebb,' he intoned with admirable restraint since, at that moment, he could have drunk a bucket of beer to himself and still have come back for more.

'Very well, here you wait; Vienna shall have her milk and you, gentlemen, I have the very thing to quench your thirst.'

He went out of the room with his cat at his heels. Todd looked at the red faces of his cronies with gleaming eyes. 'Ach now, is he no' learning fast, our stranger mannie? Wait you! He might have brought a crate o' thon strong spirits they drink in his country. You mind Anton had some sent over from Germany last New Year and everyone that had a taste o' it were falling about the island for days afterwards. Saps I think was the name he put upon it and, by jingo!, it fairly sapped the good out o' my liver. For a whole week I couldny touch the meat Mollie put on the table before me and she was that angry she near brained me wi' my plate and called me an ungrateful bodach but I was so ill I wouldny have cared if I never saw food again.'

'Schnapps that would be,' Graeme Donald corrected Todd. 'I mind o' it fine because wee Lorna McKenzie said her father was over playing a game at Anton's house and it sounded like the one she played with cards at her granny's.'

At that moment Otto came back, bearing in one hand a kettle full of hot water, in the other a tray set with eight mugs, which he placed on the coffee table near the fire. 'Now, gentlemen, if you will just come over here and make yourselves comfortable.'

Mystified, the men went to array themselves round the table, as they did so eyeing one another with raised brows and some discomfiture.

From his pocket Otto extracted four Oxo cubes. Solemnly, and with more than a little ceremony, he split them with a sharp knife and then placed half of a cube into each of the surrounding mugs. Making great play with the kettle, he held it high so that the water gushed into the cups to produce a weak brown concoction topped by frothy foam. Picking up a spoon, he proceeded to stir the beverage vigorously so that little circles of bubbles swirled around merrily.

The men swallowed hard, the expression on each face was one of misery and disappointment.

'Ay, ay now, that is indeed kind o' you,' Tam, electing himself as spokesman, muttered the words faintly while he licked his dry lips, not daring to look at the others for fear of what he would see on their faces. 'An Oxo cube is just the job on a thirsty day like this.'

'Ay, and half an Oxo cube is even better,' Ranald mouthed sarcastically, a wonder in him that anybody else could surpass himself for the meanness that he preferred to call thrift.

'Ach well, I'll get away home for a drink o' plain water.' Todd shuffled to the door. 'It will slake my thirst better than the salty stuff you have there in the cups.'

Todd must certainly have been upset as never, never had he been known to drink water which he said gave him the belly-ache. The others followed him, their footsteps as heavy as lead, the conviction growing in their hearts that 'furriners' were indeed difficult to understand with all their strange habits and customs.

An Oxo cube might be fine in Austria but on Rhanna it was unthinkable – nay, unheard of – for anyone to offer the likes to thirsty, hardworking men.

Otto looked downhearted though a smile quirked one corner of his generous mouth. 'So, you go, you do not wait for my next trick – and I had truly believed that I could persuade you to stay and drink some of this.'

With a magician-like flourish he whipped a tea-towel from an innocent-looking cardboard carton which was reposing beside the brass coal box.

At least half a dozen bottles of best malt whisky gleamed golden in the firelight, nestling beside them were a dozen bottles of beer, and, towering over everything, was an enormous flagon of schnapps with a picture of a fire-throwing dragon painted on its glazed surface.

'The *Uisge Beatha*,' Todd whispered in awe, ' enough to sink a battleship.'

'The *Uisge Beatha*?' Otto repeated questioningly.

'Tis the Gaelic for the water o' life,' Graeme explained willingly, 'and, by God!, we'll be doing the Highland Fling from Portcull to Portree once we have had some o' that golden glory safely inside us.'

'Ay, and it's no' a battleship I'll be sinking,' Tam said happily, 'it is myself who will be drowning in it and never wasting a drop in the process.'

For the next two hours they had a wonderful time. Otto played the piano for them while they got well and truly drunk, so much so that not one of them thought to question the fact that it was mainly Scottish music which flowed out from his nimble fingers.

They danced and they jigged, they hooched and they yooched while they birled one another round, faster and faster, their tackity boots thumping the floorboards and rattling the cups in the dresser.

Vienna, disturbed out of a quiet nap on Otto's bed, padded downstairs to see what all the noise was about, took one look at the wildly cavorting figures and fled.

Erchy, on his way over to Nigg with 'the mails' came up the path to deliver a letter and was soon absorbed into the happy scene. The whisky, the beer, the schnapps flowed as swiftly and as easily as the music. Todd forgot what 'the saps' had done to his liver and went about with a large glass of it in his hand shouting, '*Prost! Prost!* Drink up your saps and get lost! lost!', while everyone else cried '*Slàinte!*', which was the Gaelic for good health, to Otto, to each other, and even to the cat when at last she dared to put her little pink nose round the door.

When eventually they reeled merrily from the house there was a unanimous vote to the effect that it had been a great ceilidh and that Otto was 'the best bloody stranger ever to have set foot on Rhanna's shores,' though, when the various spouses beheld the state of their menfolk, they weren't so sure and said he must be mad or bad, or a mixture of both to encourage such goings-on in the doctor's house and all because of some ancient old piano.

It took Erchy some time to resume his rounds, mainly because he had to sit in his van for fully twenty minutes whilst he tried to ascertain the difference between the gearstick and the handbrake. When at last he was satisfied, the vehicle lurched away to an interlude of adventure. On the high cliff road to Nigg it scattered the sheep who were partial to parking themselves in the passing places. Before Erchy knew it, twenty or so sheep were stampeding along in front of him, gathering more flocks on the way so that before long there were at least fifty ewes and several lambs thundering in a terrified mass along the treacherous road.

At his first port of call, Erchy delivered old Meggie's mail to young Maisie Brown whose three children gaped at him as he tried to insert a competition leaflet into a surprised collie dog's left ear.

At the next croft he posted a letter in Aggie McKinnon's astonished mouth, informed her that that would keep her quiet for a while and also that she made a fine letter box, and went merrily on his way, feeling right pleased with himself.

Before the turn-off to Nigg, the post van veered on to the moors to take a nose-dive into a waterlogged peat bog where it settled with a soggy groan and one or two slurping wheezes. And that was where, some time later, half a dozen angry crofters, one highly indignant Aggie McKinnon and eight yapping sheepdogs found him.

As one, with the exception of Aggie who suddenly remembered she had forgotten her 'teeths' and went rushing away in embarrassment, they set about asking him 'what the hell he was playing at scattering their flocks far and wide.' They ranted and raved, the dogs barked and fought with one another and bedlam broke out on that normally deserted stretch of moorland.

Erchy heard not a thing. With his head on his mail sack, his feet on the dashboard, he was dreaming happy dreams, a most beatific smile of joy stamped firmly on his ruddy features. For some reason that would only ever be known to himself, he had, at some point, removed his socks and had affixed them to the windows, one on either side of the post van. The wind had filled them and there they blew, looking like two elongated woolly balloons, the bits of sticking plaster that covered the holes in the heels standing out like two dirty pink crosses for all the world to see.

Rachel wandered slowly along Burg Bay, lost in thought, her hands buried deep in the pockets of her green wool jacket. It was cold for early April, the wind soughed low over the Sound of Rhanna, churning up the white horses, tossing them contemptuously against the rocky outcrops which abounded in these dangerous waters. In the leaden grey of the squally sky the gulls were screaming as they fought the blustery breezes that tossed them about like bits of paper and often forced them to land on the grass-covered crags where they niggled and squabbled, or threatened one another with gaping, vicious beaks.

It was wild and windswept and wonderful. Rachel's ears tingled; her face felt the way it did on rising when she splashed it with cold water from the ewer on her dresser, fresh, alive and glowing; her hair was a mass of wind-tossed curls but she made no attempt to restrain it. The scarf that she had tied round her head before leaving the house had blown off soon afterwards and she had stood watching it as it went flapping away like a flimsy bird, soon to be lost in the marram grasses above the beach.

She wondered why she had worn it: she had always hated anything that restricted nature, but living for so long on the mainland had robbed her of many things. Jon said it had tamed her; she had laughed at that and said it had maimed her, but deep down she was still the unfettered Rachel who had wandered the wild, free lands of her beloved Rhanna and whenever she came home she gradually rid herself of the chains of convention and reverted gladly to the island ways.

Ruth had asked her to go over to Fàilte that morning but for some reason she had wanted to be alone just to think, and had promised to go over later.

She paused for a moment to gaze at the awesome spectacle of Burg rising dramatically out of the sea. Black and forbidding it was pitted with dank caverns, criss-crossed with bare ledges where seabirds nested and screamed and drifted like snowflakes in the wind that eternally battered the exposed outcrop.

Some of the basalt columns had become separated from the mother rock to form structures that looked like gigantic stepping stones and all around were the sharp, glistening fangs of the reefs piercing up out of the restless waves.

Rachel caught her lip and gave a little laugh of sheer joy. She loved it, she adored its splendour and its solitude, its grandeur and its turbulence, and at times like these she wished that she wasn't human but some drifting being who had the power to wander the wind and the storm, the oceans and the skies, for ever and ever and never feel the mortal need for human companionship and comfort.

To be human was to want, to desire, to feel loneliness and to pine after things and people that you had thought you could do without just as long as you were free to roam the wilderness and to climb the high bens where it seemed that no other footsteps but yours had trod . . .

She was missing Jon, it was as simple as that. She had needed to be alone, it had become imperative to her just to be by herself so that there was only the demands of her own body to be met and catered for; the freedom, the peace, had been wonderful, no rush, no hurry to obey the hands of the clock – there was only one clock at An Cala and she often forgot to wind it, the dawn, the day, the sun, the moon had been all the indications she had required to let her know that time was passing.

But the moments, the hours, the days of solitude had served their purpose; the silence of An Cala that had soothed her so much in the beginning was now becoming oppressive and though Jon had written to say that Mamma was on the mend and he would soon be joining her on Rhanna, it wasn't soon enough for her. Hour by hour she was becoming more and more possessed by the old restlessness and she hated herself for being mercurial and foolish but could do nothing to stop the craving for excitement that was mounting within her.

It was freezing standing there at the edge of the waves and

with an impatient sigh she began to walk up the beach towards the shelter of the dunes.

Burg Bay was vast, even with the tide coming in as it was now there was at least a quarter of a mile of shell sand and pebbly shore between the dunes and the sea. Pausing for breath, she closed her eyes for a moment. All around her was the moan of the wind and the surge of the ocean, now near, now far, pulsing, pounding, the heartbeat of the sea, mingling and merging with her own vibrantly beating heart – then she became aware of another sound, that of music, throbbing through air, time, space, powerful, passionate, compelling.

Opening her eyes, she looked up and saw the chimneys of Tigh na Cladach. She saw the blue haze of wood smoke tossing about, she smelled its piquancy and knew its delight and quickly she walked up the beach till she could see the little garden ablaze with yellow trumpets blowing in the strong breezes – the daffodils that Megan had optimistically planted and which somehow survived the spring gales.

From this house the music poured, swelling upwards in great crescendos of sound like the storm-lashed waves washing the winter shores. It was magnificent, breathtaking; Rachel stood entranced, her clenched fists held to her mouth.

Down below, a stooped, black-coated figure passed by, leading a sturdy lamb on the end of a rope. Despite all Dodie's efforts the frailest twin had died and though he had been heartbroken he had set about ensuring the health and strength of the survivor and now took it everywhere with him. It soon learned to follow him around like a faithful dog, even trotting to the wee hoosie with him when he had to obey the calls of nature.

Rachel prayed he wouldn't take it into his head to come and talk to her, this was her moment, her time, her personal private enjoyment of an experience so profound she felt the hot tears pricking her lids.

But she needn't have worried, Dodie had never been able to make much sense of her sign language – combined with his own speech difficulties it was all just too much for him. If by chance they did meet he was wont to shuffle his feet awkwardly or simply stand and stare at her as if he expected some miracle might restore her speech at any moment.

He glanced up and saw her and the familiar '*Tha brèeah!*' filtered to her thinly on the wind before he went on his way, his long coat flapping behind him like one of Ranald's vampires.

She let go her breath, then, as if drawn by a magnet, she followed the music to its source, opening the little gate set into the sturdy dyke that took so many batterings from the high, winter seas it had to be repaired every year. Tiptoeing to the window, she stood with her back to the wall and let the waves of glorious sound soak into her.

So enthralled was she, she wasn't aware that the music had stopped till the door in the solid stone porch was wrenched open and Herr Otto Klebb stood framed in the aperture, his head thrust forward to avoid banging it, having learned to his cost that he was too tall to go through the opening in the normal way.

But to her it was a sign of aggression and she stared at him, her heart beating swiftly in her breast, all the sophistication and poise that had been hers for so long falling away in one short burst of apprehension so that she was left feeling like a small child who had been caught in the act of doing something that was naughty and forbidden.

Chapter Eight

Otto said nothing, instead, and without ado, he reached for her hand and pulled her inside, straight to the sitting room where he spun her round to face him, his expression dark and forbidding.

Rachel held her breath; she didn't want to feel like this, embarrassed, silly, utterly devoid of the pride that had always made her hold her head high, no matter the circumstances. She had felt more confidence on the concert platform, facing an audience of hundreds, than she did standing before this man who, in just a few short minutes, had robbed her of everything that had taken her years to master.

Yet fierce as he appeared to her now, he had already endeared himself in the hearts of those islanders who had crossed his path. Tam and his cronies were full of him and they had forced everyone else to be full of him too. The tale of the ceilidh, his generosity and the wonderful Scottish music that had flowed effortlessly from his clever fingers had spread far and wide. He had become Mr Mystery Man Number One, and those who had walked on Burg Bay had been enchanted by the music pouring from the shorehouse, for, as well as the piano, Otto was accompanied by a full orchestral backing, using the tapes that he had brought with him to Rhanna.

'It is like having a symphony concert on our very own doorstep,' Barra McLean had enthused, even while something about Otto tugged at her memory. But for the moment she couldn't quite think what that something was, and as she was a connoisseur of good music, she was quite content to enjoy Otto's playing while she could. Later she might remember where she had seen him before, if indeed she had seen him at all.

As far as everyone else was concerned he was just a man who happened to have an excellent talent for the piano, and though the kind of music he played wasn't everyone's cup of tea, the passion and the power of it enthralled them anyway and fitted in well with the wild, romantic setting of lonely Burg Bay.

And now Rachel had heard that music for herself and had been even more appreciative than anyone, but she hadn't bargained for an outcome of this nature and wished she hadn't been so foolish as to venture near the house.

She wanted to turn her head away in order to avoid the questions in his penetrating gaze, but no, she wasn't going to let him see how much he had startled her! So she met his eyes with her own and as she looked at him fully for the first time awareness accelerated her already fast-beating heart. This man was no ordinary stranger! She knew who he was – he wasn't Otto Klebb, he was Karl Gustav Langer, world-renowned concert pianist and composer, who had played in all the great concert halls of the world.

He had composed modern classical music, for orchestra, films, and the stage and he had made recordings of all his own works as well as the great classical works of Mozart, Beethoven, Brahms and many others. Rachel had attended one of his concerts some years ago; she had been very young but she had never forgotten the experience, it was imprinted in her memory, both the music and the man.

One of her greatest ambitions had been to play with him on the concert platform. She had played solo parts with many great symphony orchestras throughout the world but she had never achieved her ambition to play with Karl Langer, perhaps because he hadn't been heard of so much in recent years. It had been rumoured that he had retired because of ill health; other sources said he had been weighed down by private and personal worries and had bowed out of the limelight only temporarily. Whatever the cause he had disappeared from the world stage – and now here he was, the great maestro and teacher, standing before her as large as life and twice as forbidding, his eyes raking her face as if he was trying to read her mind.

And he did, quite brutally, as if he blamed her personally for having found out his identity. 'You know who I am,' he growled, a look of thunder darkening his brow. 'I expected this moment of truth but I didn't wish it to happen so soon and particularly when I was just beginning to enjoy my anonymity. When I encountered you at the harbour and saw the look on your face I knew that it would only be a matter of time before you recognized me. Tina told me who you were and I cursed the fates that put us on this island at the same time. Rachel Jodl, the beautiful, young violinist, already attaining dizzy heights on the international concert stage. Unable to speak but saying it all through music. You see, I know all about you, I have heard your name spoken amongst the stars; little did I think I would bump into you on a remote Hebridean island.'

She wanted to ask him so many things – why he had chosen Rhanna as his hideaway, where he had gleaned his knowledge about Scotland, why he was so interested in the McKinnons. She also wanted to shout at him, to tell him that she belonged here on this island, that her heart and spirit were rooted in the very soil from which she had sprung, but nothing, of course, would come out, only a very faint sobbing sound that was her soul trying to be heard.

He studied her and he wondered if she knew how beautiful she looked with her wind-tossed black curls framing her face. The bracing air had made the roses bloom in her satin-smooth cheeks, her tall young body was graceful and sweet yet there was such an air of sensuality about her that it tantalized and teased and seemed to beckon, and all without any effort on her part. And those eyes – black and hectic with the life forces that he knew were churning inside her – at that moment they also flashed with anger, frustration and a hundred questions waiting to be answered.

Again he seemed to read her mind and a wry smile twisted his mouth. 'You and I, *mein Frau*, have come to this island for the same reasons: to rest, to recharge the batteries, to be the free spirits we can never be in public with a thousand eyes watching us. My time here will be short – six months – a year if I am lucky. I have much to do before my stay is up, I have come on a journey of discovery, a pilgrimage if you like. It will be a summer of sadness and of joy – but I go too quickly. All in the course of time, as I keep telling my good friend, Herr Tam. I only ask you not to give my little secret away. Karl Langer belongs to the world; Otto Klebb belongs on this island, everyone knows me as such.'

Then he bent and kissed her, so suddenly she had no chance to take evasive action. His mouth was firm and warm and passionate, she didn't struggle or move away, she was too mesmerized by the events of the morning to be surprised at any further happenings, and – something else – she was stunned and thrilled at being kissed by this man, the charismatic stranger who had turned out to be the maestro, the admired and adored Karl Gustav Langer. Famous as she herself was, it wasn't every day that she found herself being kissed by someone of his calibre and she allowed him to kiss her, deeper and deeper till he let her go as abruptly as he had claimed her.

He smiled at the look on her face. 'Your mouth needed that kiss as much as mine did. Don't worry, it will not happen too often, only when you tempt me beyond endurance. I am aware of your married status, Frau Rachel, and I am not the sort to come between a man and his wife.'

For the first time in his presence she smiled, the radiance of it lighting her face.

He nodded. 'I will tell you what you must have heard a hundred, no – a thousand times, your smile, it is enchanting, a delight to behold, your face in repose haunts the heart, and as I have no desire to be haunted by you or anyone else, I wish for you to keep on your face, the smile. Ah, little Rachel, if only you could speak to me, this conversation is very one-sided. Show me something, some gesture, some word, that will let me know what you are feeling, thinking.'

She reddened, communication with those who didn't under-stand the signals of her hands always seemed so hopeless and